Dear Reader,

My Mysteria novellas grew from two of my favorite things: wine and
Gena Showalter (though not necessarily in that order!). Gena and I have
been friends for years. I can't remember exactly which RT Booklovers
Convention we were at (lack of memory attributed to the wine), but it was
during some heavy "working" at the RT bar that Gena and I came up with
the idea to create a magical town—somewhere gorgeous, like Colorado—
where our characters, especially our heroines, could interact with each other
and have fun, funny, and sexy adventures. This RT convention was so long
ago that Gena and I were scrambling to pay for the convention (and the
wine), our room (which we shared—Gena was a good roommate, except she
shed like a cat), and food (and drink). The reason this little financial fact is
important is because if we hadn't been stuck together in a hotel room, we
probably never would have followed through on our alcohol-soaked anthology idea. Well, we sobered up and wrote an outline, a world bible, and a
proposal for Mysteria. I then sent everything to my longtime editor at
Berkley, Christine Zika, having no clue that Berkley had never before published an author-incepted romance anthology. Get this: Berkley bought
the idea! Gena and I did a bunch of high-fiving and then got down to the
business of playing in each other's literary sandboxes.

　　Guess what happened? We had an awesome time! The novellas Gena
and I created still make me giggle. Writing is a solitary profession; it
really is magic when authors get the opportunity to work together on proj-
ects, especially when the authors are good friends. I think you'll appreciate
what we created. May our combined awesome times bring you giggles,
too, and maybe your own little glimmer of magic.

Happy reading,
P. C. Cast

Stay tuned for Gena's novellas, which will
continue the Mysteria fantasy and fun!

PRAISE FOR THE NOVELS OF P. C. CAST

"Sexy, charming, and fun, *Goddess of Love* is the fantasy romance of the year! You will fall in love with this book. (I did!)"
—Susan Grant, *New York Times* bestselling author

"Ms. Cast has taken mythology, Cinderella, a bit of Shakespeare, and a dash of Shaw and mixed them with her own style of comedy for a winning read that is [as] heartwarming as it is funny." —*Huntress Book Reviews*

"Most innovative . . . From beginning to end, the surprises in P. C. Cast's new page-turner never stopped. Its poignancy resonates with both whimsy and fantasy . . . I loved it!" —Sharon Sala, *New York Times* bestselling author

"An amusingly tongue-in-cheek take on the Trojan War featuring a modern-day heroine . . . Funny, irreverent, and clever . . . You can't go wrong."
—*The Romance Reader*

"Outstanding . . . Magic, myth, and romance with a decidedly modern twist. Her imagination and storytelling abilities are true gifts to the genre."
—*RT Book Reviews*

"Pure enjoyment . . . Anything can [happen] when gods and mortals mix."
—*Rendezvous*

"A fanciful mix of mythology and romance with a dash of humor for good measure . . . Engages and entertains . . . Lovely." —*Romance Reviews Today*

"One of the top romantic-fantasy mythologists today." —*Midwest Book Review*

"Captivating—poignant, funny, erotic! Lovely characters, wonderful romance, constant action, and a truly whimsical fantasy . . . Delightful. A great read."
—*The Best Reviews*

"A fun combination of myth, girl power, and sweet romance [with] a bit of suspense. A must-read . . . A romance that celebrates the magic of being a woman."
—*Affaire de Coeur*

ACCIDENTAL MAGIC

P. C. Cast

Previously published in *Mysteria Nights,*
Mysteria Lane, and *Mysteria.*

BERKLEY SENSATION, NEW YORK

THE BERKLEY PUBLISHING GROUP
Published by the Penguin Group
Penguin Group (USA) Inc.
375 Hudson Street, New York, New York 10014, USA

Penguin Group (Canada), 90 Eglinton Avenue East, Suite 700, Toronto, Ontario M4P 2Y3, Canada
(a division of Pearson Penguin Canada Inc.) • Penguin Books Ltd., 80 Strand, London WC2R 0RL,
England • Penguin Group Ireland, 25 St. Stephen's Green, Dublin 2, Ireland (a division of Penguin
Books Ltd.) • Penguin Group (Australia), 250 Camberwell Road, Camberwell, Victoria 3124, Australia
(a division of Pearson Australia Group Pty. Ltd.) • Penguin Books India Pvt. Ltd., 11 Community
Centre, Panchsheel Park, New Delhi—110 017, India • Penguin Group (NZ), 67 Apollo Drive,
Rosedale, Auckland 0632, New Zealand (a division of Pearson New Zealand Ltd.) • Penguin Books
(South Africa) (Pty.) Ltd., 24 Sturdee Avenue, Rosebank, Johannesburg 2196, South Africa

Penguin Books Ltd., Registered Offices: 80 Strand, London WC2R 0RL, England

This is a work of fiction. Names, characters, places, and incidents either are the product of the author's
imagination or are used fictitiously, and any resemblance to actual persons, living or dead, business
establishments, events, or locales is entirely coincidental. The publisher does not have any control over
and does not assume any responsibility for author or third-party websites or their content.

Novellas previously published in *Mysteria Nights*, *Mysteria Lane*, and *Mysteria*.

"Introduction" by P. C. Cast copyright © 2006 by P. C. Cast.
"Candy Cox and the Big Bad (Were)Wolf" by P. C. Cast copyright © 2006 by P. C. Cast.
"It's in His Kiss" by P. C. Cast copyright © 2008 by P. C. Cast.
Excerpt from *Goddess of Legend* by P. C. Cast copyright © 2010 by P. C. Cast.
Cover design by SDG Concepts.

PUBLISHING HISTORY
Berkley Sensation trade paperback edition / September 2012

Library of Congress Cataloging-in-Publication Data

Cast, P. C.
Accidental magic / P. C. Cast.
p. cm.
1. Divorced women—Fiction.   2. Vegetarians—Fiction.   3. Werewolves—Fiction.
4. Magic—Fiction.   5. Vampires—Fiction.   6. Paranormal romance stories.   I. Title.
PS3603.A869A33 2012   2012022743
813'.6—dc22

PRINTED IN THE UNITED STATES OF AMERICA

10 9 8 7 6 5 4 3 2 1

CONTENTS

INTRODUCTION

Once upon a time in a land closer than anyone might be comfortable with, a demon high lord was sent to destroy a small, starving (and, let's face it, weird) band of settlers who were fleeing the last town they'd tried to settle in (a place eventually known as Kansas City, Missouri, the Show Me State, which did indeed show them tar and feathers and the road west). The group was composed of magical misfits and outcasts: a bloodaphobic vampire, a black-magic witch and her white-magic husband, a pack of amorous (translation: hump-happy) werewolves, and a man named John, who had gotten confused and joined the wrong wagon train. When the demon spied this ragged, rejected bunch, he (for a reason known only to himself but which had to do with uncontrollable random acts of kindness) decided not just to spare them but to create a magical haven for them.

And so, nestled in a beautiful valley in the Rocky Mountains, the town of Mysteria was founded. Over the years, it became a refuge for creatures of the night and those unwanted by traditional society. No one—or thing—was turned away. Magic thrived, aphrodisiacs laced the pollen, and fairy tales came true.

The first settlers eventually died (those that weren't already dead or undead, that is), but they left pieces of themselves behind. The vampire invented a powerful blood-appetite suppressant for any other vampires with a fear of blood. The witch and the warlock created a wishing well—a wishing well that swirled and churned with both white and black magic, a dangerous combination. The hump-happy werewolves left the essence of perpetual springtime and love (translation: they peed all around the boundary of the city, so that everyone—or thing—that entered or left Mysteria was, well, marked). John, the only nonmagical being in the group, left his confused but mundane genes, founding a family that would ultimately spawn more humans of nonmagical abilities who remained in Mysteria because finding their way out was just too much like geometry.

Each of the settlers thought, as their spirits floated to the heavens—all right, some of them went straight to hell, the naughty sinners—that their best contribution to the fantastical town of Mysteria was a happily-ever-after for their descendants. If only they could have known the events that would one day unfold . . .

* ✳ *

CANDY COX
AND THE BIG BAD
(WERE)WOLF

For S.L.,
with a smile and a wink.
Thanks for the . . . inspiration.

ACKNOWLEDGMENTS

I'd like to thank Berkley, and especially my talented editor, Christine Zika, for publishing this author-created anthology. It's wonderful when your publisher believes in you.

Thank you to my agent and friend, Meredith Bernstein, who said, "Absolutely!" when I called her with this idea.

And a big THANKS GIRLFRIENDS to Gena Showalter (my partner in crime in the inception of this anthology), Susan Grant, and MaryJanice Davidson. It was such fun to work on this with the three of you. Let's do it again soon!

✳ 1 ✳

"Godiva! Wait—wait—wait. Did you just say that you and your sisters called forth the dead two nights ago?" Candice said, rubbing her forehead where it was beginning to ache.

"Yeah, but you missed the important part. Romeo was . . . *spectacular*," Godiva said breathlessly into the phone. "Who knew that poor, wounded wolf would turn into something—I mean, some*one*—so delectable."

"So he actually did more than hump your leg this time?"

"Candy Cox—I swear you haven't been listening."

"You know I hate it when you call me that."

"Fine. *Candice*, you haven't been listening," Godiva said.

"He's not just a wolf. He's a *were*wolf, which means he has an excellent tongue and he humps a lot more than my leg."

Candice kept muttering as if Godiva hadn't spoken. "It's not like I don't get enough of that name crap at school. Why I ever decided to attempt to teach high school morons I'll never know." She cringed inwardly, remembering the countless times some hormone-impaired sixteen-year-old boy had made a wise-ass remark (usually replete with sophomoric clichés) about her name. God, she was truly sick and tired of Mysteria High School—Home of the Fighting Fairies.

"You could have kept one of your ex-husbands' names," Godiva said helpfully.

"Oh, please," Candice scoffed. "I'd rather sound like a porn star than keep any reminders of ex-husband numbers one through five. No. My solution is to change careers. As soon as I finish my online master's in creative writing I can dump the fucking Fighting Fairies and snag that job in Denver as assistant editor for Full Moon Press."

"Honey, have I told you lately that you have a very nasty mouth for a schoolteacher?"

"Yes. And I do believe I've told you that I *have* said nasty mouth *because* I'm a schoolteacher. Uh, please. Shall we take a moment to recall the one and only day you subbed for me?"

Godiva shuddered. "Ack! Do not remind me. I take back any form of criticism for your coarse language. Those teenagers are worse than a whole assortment of wraiths, demons, and undead. I mean, really, some of them even smell worse!" Just remembering had her making an automatic retching sound. "But Candice, seriously, I don't want you to move!"

"Denver's not that far away—we shop till we drop there several times a year. You know I need a change. The teenage monsters are wearing on me."

"I know," Godiva sighed. Then she brightened. "Hey! I could work on a spell that might help shut those boys up whenever they try to speak your name. Maybe something to do with testicles and tiny brains . . ."

"That's really sweet of you, but you know that magic doesn't work on or around me, so it probably wouldn't work on my name, either." Candice sighed. It was true. As a descendant of one of the few nonmagical founders of the town (his name was, appropriately, John Smith), Candice had No Magic at All. Yes, sadly, she lived in a town full of witches, warlocks, vampires, fairies, werewolves, et cetera, et cetera, and her magic was nonmagic. It figured. Her magic worked like her marriages. Not at all. "Men are such a pain in the ass."

Without losing a beat at her friend's sudden change in subjects, Godiva giggled. "I agree completely, which is why I know exactly what you need—a werewolf lover."

"Godiva Tawdry! I'm too damn old to roll around the woods with a dog."

"A werewolf is not a dog. And forty is not old. Plus, you look ten years younger. Why do you think high school boys still get crushes on you, *Ms. Candy Cox?*"

"Put boobs on a snake and high school boys would chase after it. And don't call me Candy."

Godiva laughed. "True, but that doesn't make you any less attractive. You've got a killer body, Ms. Cox."

"I'm fat."

"You're curvy."

"I'm old."

"You're ripe."

"Godiva! Do you not remember what happened last time I let myself commit matrimony?"

"Clearly," Godiva said. "It took ex-husband number five less than six months to almost bore you to death. And he seemed like such a nice guy."

"Yes, I admit he did seem nice. They all did at first." Candice sighed. "Who knew that he would literally almost kill me? And after my brush with death, I decided that I. Am. Done."

"Okay, look. You accidentally took an unhealthy mixture of Zoloft, Xanax, and pinot grigio. It could happen to anyone, especially when she's being bored to death by a man scratching himself while he incessantly flips from the History Channel to CNN—"

"—And pops Viagra like they're M&Ms and thinks that the telltale oh-so-attractive capillary flush constitutes foreplay,"

Candice interrupted. "Yeesh. I'm going to just say no from here on out. Truly. I've sworn off men."

"No, I remember exactly what you said. 'Godiva'—here you raised your fist to the sky like Scarlett O'Hara—'I will never marry again.' So you've sworn off marriage, not men. And anyway, a werewolf is not technically a man. Or at least if he is, it's only for part of the time. The rest of the time he is the most adorably cuddly sweet furry—"

"Fine." Candice cut off Godiva's gushing. "I'll think about it."

"Really?"

"Yes." *No,* she thought. She hurried on before Godiva could press the point. "I've really gotta go. I'm deep in the middle of Homework Hell. I have to turn in my poetry collection to the online creative writing professor next week, and I still haven't figured out a theme for the damn thing. I'm totally screwed if I can't get rid of this writer's block."

"Well . . ." Godiva giggled mischievously. "I don't know how it'd work on writer's block, but Romeo sure unclogged me last night."

"You're not helping."

"I'm just saying—a little werewolf action might fix you right up."

"You're still not helping."

"Sorry. I'll let you get back to your writing. Remember, you said you'd think about a werewolf lover."

"Yeah, I'll think about it right after I think about my poetry theme. Uh, shouldn't you and your sisters be frolicking about the graveyard checking on the dead or whatnot?"

"Oh, don't worry about it. Our little screwup actually ended up being a good thing, what with those horrid demons on the prowl; the town could use the extra protection. And anyway, it's only temporary and the dead have already quieted down. Uh, but since you mentioned it . . . are you planning on going jogging today?"

"Yes."

"Do you think you could take a spin through the graveyard and keep your eyes open for my broom? I must have forgotten it in all the excitement that night, between Genevieve scampering off into the woods with Hunter—whose eyes, by the way, were glowing bright red—and my Romeo morphing from wolf to man rather unexpectedly. Anyway, if you see it would you please grab it before somebody flies off with it? You know a good broom is hard to find."

"Yeah, sure. If I see it, I'll get it for you. But wait, isn't Hunter Knight supposed to be dead?" Candice said.

"Well, kinda. Actually, he's a little undead."

"Isn't that like being a little pregnant?"

"Don't be a smart-ass. It's embarrassing enough for me to admit that my sister's getting some vampire action. God, I wish the girl had better taste in men, alive or dead."

Candice sighed. "Hey—don't be such a prude. If I'd chosen one of the undead I might not be unmarried."

"Candice, honey, I love you, but you are a hopeless piece of work. Now be a doll and go find my broom. Bye."

Godiva hung up the phone and sat tapping her chin with one long, slender finger. Candy was getting old before her time. Goddess knew, she really did need a lover. A young lover. A young werewolf lover. A hot, naughty affair would be the perfect thing to keep her from moving to Denver. Her fingers itched to swirl up a little love spell, but magic wouldn't work on her friend. Godiva's eyes widened and her full, pink lips tilted up. Magic wouldn't work on Candy, but it definitely would work on a werewolf. . . .

✳ 2 ✳

Candice would never get this damn assignment done.

"You'd think after teaching for almost twenty years I wouldn't have any problem doing homework." She grumbled at herself and ran a frustrated hand through her thick blonde hair. "Poetry themes . . . poetry themes . . . poetry themes . . ." Death, time, love, heartbreak, the soul, happiness, sex . . . "Sex," she muttered, chewing the end of her well-sharpened #2 pencil. "That's one I can't write about. Like I've had sex in—"

She clamped her lips shut, refusing to speak aloud the ridiculous amount of time it had been since the last time she'd been laid. As if the last time even counted. Ex-husband number five had been, in politically correct terms, penis impaired. Spoken plainly, he'd had a pathetically small dick, and an incredibly large wallet. Unfortunately, one did not make up for the other. Candice grimaced. Quite frankly, women who said size didn't count had clearly never been with a man with a small dick. And, as if their, well, lack of substance wasn't bad enough, SDM (small-dicked men) had the same problems short men had. They were mad at the world. Like it *helped* to make up for said unfortunate shortage by being a jerk? Sometimes men just didn't make sense.

"Theme!" she said, forcing her thoughts back to the blank notebook page. She wanted to create poetry that would dazzle her professor, replete with complex symbolism, witty phrasing, and possibly even a few clever slant rhymes. What she had come up with was exactly—she glanced at the naked page—nothing.

She was, indeed, screwed (figuratively speaking).

"Okay, so write something . . . anything . . . write what you know. . . ."

What the hell did she know? She knew she was sick of teaching the Fighting Fairies and she knew she would never get married again. Well, she certainly didn't want to write about high school, which left . . .

"What the hell. At least it'll get me writing."

She drew a deep breath and let her pencil begin moving across the blank page.

Keep your Errol Flynns, Paul Newmans, Mel Gibsons
all puppets—empty masquerades.

She blinked and reread the first two lines. Not Shakespeare, but it did have a certain ring to it. Candice grinned and continued.

Tom, Dick, and Harry, too
the boy next door
I want no more.

Wasn't that the truth! Her pencil, with a mind of its own, kept moving.

You ask, what now?
Well,

And the self-propelled pencil stubbornly stopped. What now? What now? What now? She jumped as the clock in her study chimed seven times. Seven o'clock already? How long had she been on the phone with Godiva? Now she'd have to hurry to get in her five-mile jog, complete with graveyard detour, before the sun set. Crap! She absolutely didn't want to be outside alone after dusk. Weird things had been going on around town lately—and it took some doing for anything to be classified as "weird" by a Mysteria native. Candice put down her pencil and began pulling on her running shoes.

The beat of her shoes against the blacktop road was a seductive lure. The sound beckoned to him. He'd heard it while he was still deep in the woods. It had called him away from the young thing he was still licking. She snarled after him, disgruntled and unsatisfied at his premature departure. He called a hasty apology and promised to meet her and her twin sister later. Right now he had to follow the beat of her running feet, even though it was unlike him to leave such a delicious tidbit. He prided himself on his ability to satisfy. Like a modern Don Juan, his lovers could count on him for romancing as well as consistent orgasming, but the steady slapping sound seemed to somehow have gotten into his body. It pulled him away from his lover with an incredibly powerful singularity in thought.

You (beat) need (beat) her (beat). You (beat) can't (beat) stay (beat) away (beat).

The rhythmic lure thrummed with his pulse . . . his heartbeat . . . it pounded through his loins, making them feel hot and heavy. He scented the warm evening breeze. Woman . . . hot, sweaty, and ripe. And not far ahead of him. He wanted her with a single-minded intensity that he hadn't felt for anything or anyone in years. Growling deep in his throat, he hurried to catch her.

Jeesh, gross. Candice kept glancing nervously from side to side as she sprinted through the graveyard, totally annoyed that she'd promised Godiva she'd look for her broom. Not slowing down, she gritted her teeth and peered into the creepy shadows that flitted past the edge of her vision. Nope. No broom. Also no walking corpses, trolls, goblins, or fairies (whom she disliked with an intensity she knew was unreasonable—they hadn't asked to be made the school mascot and she shouldn't hold it against them, but she did). Nothing untoward at all. Just lots of spooky graves and silence. Thank God. Sometimes it was damn disconcerting to be normal in a town filled with abnormals. She shivered and increased her pace, wanting to leave the graveyard and (hopefully) anything that wasn't 100 percent human behind her.

Lengthening her stride, Candice thought that the burn in her muscles actually felt good. Godiva had been right about one thing—she did have a killer body. Sure, she'd like to lose a few pounds. Who wouldn't? But thanks to her lifelong love of jogging, her legs were long and strong. She also still had excellent boobs. No, they weren't as perky as they had been a few years ago, but they were full and womanly, without boulder-hard, anatomically impossible enhancements. And—best of all—she had seriously big blonde hair that was light enough to hide the encroaching gray without requiring too many touch-ups.

With a burst of speed, she shot out of the graveyard and pounded down the empty blacktop road that would eventually circle around and lead back to her house, which had been built, log-cabin style, at the edge of town. Maybe she could keep up this pace the rest of the way home. Hell, she might even run an extra mile or so!

Which was a lovely thought until the cramp hit her right calf.

"Shit!" She pulled up. Hobbling like Quasimodo she looked around for anything that might resemble sanctuary. Breathing a sigh of relief, she realized that the little rise in the road was the bridge that covered Wolf Creek. She could sit on the bank and rub her calf back into working order. So much for sprinting home.

She had just pulled off her shoe and thick athletic sock when she heard the growl. Low and deep it drifted to her on the breeze, tickling up her spine. It sounded too big to be a dog. It was probably a werewolf. Sometimes the damn things were thick as rabbits in the mountains around Mysteria. Candice rubbed harder at the cramp. She wasn't actually afraid. Werewolves were rarely more than annoying. They tended to come and go in packs—unerringly drawn to the town's preternatural nature, but except for a couple of gainfully employed families (surprisingly, werewolves tended to be excellent restaurateurs—must have something to do with the whole pack mentality and their love of meat or whatever) they usually didn't stick around long, and didn't interact with Mysteria residents, especially while they were in their wolf forms. They certainly didn't pose a danger, unless one was made nervous by big dogs. Candice didn't mind big dogs (as evidenced by her choice in ex-husbands one and two).

"Did you hurt yourself?"

His voice was deep, with a rough, husky sound that was very much man, not wolf. She swiveled around in time to see him step from the edge of the pine trees. And her mouth flopped unattractively open. He was easily six-foot-four and probably 230 pounds. At least. Broad shoulders seemed to stretch on forever, and a wide, scrumptious chest tapered down to a well-defined waist. And those legs . . . even through the relaxed jeans she could see that they were lean and muscular. His face was in shadow, so all of her attention focused on his body and the way he stalked toward her with a strong, feral grace that made her breath catch and her mouth go dry.

Then, as if he'd walked into an invisible tree, he stopped. He hesitated, and seemed almost confused. She could see him run his hand through his hair. He wore it long and loose and it framed his shadowy face as if he was an ancient warrior god that had only partially materialized in the modern world.

"Ms. Cox?"

"Yes!" she said on a burst of breath, totally surprised that the warrior god knew her name.

"It's me, Justin."

He started toward her again, and she blinked up at him as

his face emerged from the shadows. And what a face it was! Strong, well-defined cheekbones and a rugged, masculine chin. His sand-colored hair was thick, with a sexy, mussed curl. His eyes . . . his eyes were an unusual shade of amber and were almost as inviting as his beautiful mouth.

"Justin Woods. You know . . ." He hesitated, then flashed an endearingly warm smile that was just the right mixture of mischievous and nervous. ". . . I had you for sophomore English."

She mentally recoiled. What the hell had he just said? An ex-student! So the warrior god was really a fucking Fighting Fairy. Didn't it just figure? Candice frowned, trying to pull her thoughts from the bedroom into the classroom.

"Oh, that's right. Wow. Time sure flies," she said with forced levity, feeling suddenly old and as out of date as an eight-track tape. She looked up at him, shielding her eyes from the setting sun with her hand. Yep. She vaguely recognized the echo of the gawky teenager within the man. "What was that, five years ago?"

"More like ten." He crouched next to her and nodded at her bare leg. "Did you hurt yourself?" he repeated.

"Oh, no. It's nothing. Just a cramp." He was so close to her that she could feel the heat of his body and smell him—young and virile and masculine. Holy shit, he was one wickedly sexy young man!

"I can fix that," he said. "I like to jog and I'm prone to leg cramps, especially when it's hot out like this. I know just what to do to make it go away."

Without waiting for her to respond he took her foot and propped it in his lap. Then he began to massage her cramping calf. His hands were strong and his touch was warm and experienced.

"Lie back. Relax." His voice had dropped to the deep, throaty tone he'd used when he'd first come into the clearing. "Let me take care of you."

She stared at him. She should tell him to take her foot out of his crotch and take his hands off her leg. But his touch was doing the most amazing things to her body. His fingers were sending little ripples of shock from her calf up the inside of her thigh and directly to her crotch, filling her with an unexpected rush of heat and wetness.

"Don't fight it. There's no reason to. It's just me," he said. His breath had deepened and his eyes kept traveling from her mouth to her breasts. She glanced down at herself and saw that her aroused nipples were clearly visible through her damp T-shirt and sheer white sports bra.

What would it hurt? It had been years since a beautiful young man had rubbed anything on her body. Years . . .

The thought of realistically just how many years it had been since a man this young had touched her had Candice sitting straight up and pulling her tingling leg from his warm hands.

She flexed her foot and refused to meet his eyes as she pulled on her sock.

"Thanks!" she said with considerably more perkiness than she felt. "That's fine. Good as new."

"Well, at least now I know how you stay in such great shape."

"Yeah, that's me. Miss Great Shape." She cringed. Miss Great Shape? What the hell was she saying?

"I had a huge crush on you in high school," he murmured.

Her eyes widened with surprise and finally lifted to meet his. He had leaned back on his elbow and he was watching her with an intent expression that was anything but boylike.

"I thought you were the sexiest woman I'd ever seen," he said.

Candice was trapped by his frank, masculine appraisal, and the fact that he clearly liked what he saw. Her mouth felt dry and she couldn't seem to find her voice.

"You're still the sexiest woman I've ever seen."

She felt excitement slither low and hot through her belly. Lord, he was delicious! Her gaze slid from his beautiful eyes to his lips. He smiled, confident and handsome and just a little bit teasingly.

Candice blinked. *Reality, girl! Snap the fuck out of it!*

"You shouldn't say things like that," she said in her best teacher voice, forcing her gaze from his lips and pulling on her shoe.

"Why not?"

"Because you're my ex-student!" she blurted.

He flashed the smile again and scooted forward. Brushing her hands gently aside, he began slowly tying her shoe.

"I'm of age. Well of age. I'm twenty-six."

"Twenty-six!" Her voice sounded shrill. "I thought you were twenty-seven." As if one year actually made a difference. He was an infant! Practically a teenager.

"I'll be twenty-seven if you want me to be," he added huskily.

"Uh, no. A year really doesn't make that much difference." Thank God, he was done tying her shoe. Candice started to stand, only to feel his strong hands under her elbows as he helped her to her feet.

"I agree with you. A few years don't make much difference."

He kept his hands on her arms, holding her close to him. He smelled so damned good. She could feel his thumbs rubbing slow, soft circles above her elbows. That simple caress spread electric sensation from her arms all the way down to her crotch. He was wearing a plain gray T-shirt, worn thin and soft by many washings. The outline of his chest was clearly visible beneath it. He was strong and firm and deliciously big. She wanted to lean into him and lick him through the damn shirt. And then bite him. Yeah, she'd like to nibble her way down his body.

What the fuck am I thinking? She stumbled back out of the seductive cocoon of his arms.

"Our age difference is more than a few years, Justin." She tried for her teacher voice again. Unfortunately she sounded more like a breathless Marilyn Monroe.

He shrugged broad shoulders and grinned at her. "You're really cute about that."

"About what?" Her mind didn't seem to be processing correctly, and she inanely added, "And I'm not cute."

"About our age difference. And you are cute about this one thing. Other than that you're sexy and beautiful." He brushed a strand of thick blonde hair that had escaped from her ponytail out of her face. "May I walk you home?"

Candice batted at his hand. "No, you may not."

"Why not? And don't say it's because I'm too young. My age should work for me when it comes to walking." He grinned and added, "Or jogging. I don't imagine many older men can keep up with you."

"Actually, they can't," she said. Despite herself she was thoroughly enjoying their flirty banter.

"Just as I thought! So there's no reason why I can't walk you home."

"Yes, there is. I've sworn off men," she said firmly.

He threw his head back and laughed, a sound that was as seductively masculine as it was youthfully exuberant.

"That's perfect, because I'm not a man."

"Exactly the problem," she countered, finding that she was unable to keep herself from smiling in response. "You're a boy, and I don't go out walking with boys."

His amber eyes darkened. With a quick movement that was feral in its grace he closed the space that had grown between them. He took her hand in his and, without his eyes leaving hers, he turned it over, palm up, and kissed her at the pulse point on her wrist. His lips were so close to her skin when he spoke that they brushed her arm, making her shiver with the warmth of his breath. "I'm no boy." Then, eyes shining, he nipped her gently. "But I am a werewolf. So you can go out walking with me—or anything else you might like to do—and still be sworn off men."

✳ 3 ✳

What harm could letting him walk her home cause? It wasn't like he was a stranger, and he was right. He wasn't a teenager anymore. Really. He was twenty-six. And a half.

Plus, she was having fun. Justin was making her laugh with stories about botched meat deliveries at his family's restaurant, Red Riding Hood's Steak and Ale House, which bragged it was "the best darn steak place this side of Denver." She hadn't remembered him as being this charming or witty in high school. Little wonder—the only thing more self-absorbed and boorish than teenage boys were teenage girls.

Laughing, she made squeamish noises as he finished the

story about the fist-sized hunk of fur that had been found in a package of ground buffalo meat, and how his dad hadn't figured out that it was really buffalo fur and not wolf fur until after he'd sheared the pelts off of each of his brothers.

"Thankfully, I was out of town on one of my many buying trips for the restaurant." He rubbed a hand through his thick hair. "I know it grows back, but still . . ."

"So, that's what you do? You work at your family's restaurant?"

"Yeah."

"Do you like it?"

"I guess."

She studied his handsome face, wondering at the sudden change in his attitude. And then an old memory surfaced. "Wait! Aren't you an artist? Don't I remember you winning the PTA Reflections Contest at the state level your sophomore year?"

He moved his shoulder and looked uncomfortable. "That was a long time ago. I don't do much art anymore."

"Why not? I remember that you were very talented."

"Just lost interest. It started to feel like just another chore—like washing dishes at the restaurant. Whatever." Then he seemed to mentally shake himself and his expression brightened. "Enough about that. I want to hear about you. So you're still teaching?"

"Not for much longer, I hope," she said.

He laughed. "How are you going to escape from the Fighting Fairies?"

"Ironically, through education. I'm working on my MFA. As soon as I finish it, I'm off to Denver to snag a job as an editor."

"Well, it'll be the Fairies' loss."

"Right now it doesn't feel like the Fairies need to worry. I'm in the middle of a poetry class that's trying to kill me; sometimes I don't think I'll ever get through it."

"Really?" He rubbed his chin, amber eyes shining. "Let's see if I remember. . . ." He cleared his throat and gave a quick, nervous laugh.

She raised her brows questioningly. What was he up to? Then he began a recitation. At first he spoke the lines hesitantly, but as he continued his confidence grew.

If it be sin to love, and hold one heart,
Far 'mongst the stars above, supreme, apart,
If it be sin to deeply cherish one,
And hold her rich and rare as beams the sun
Across the morning skies,
Then have I sinned, but sinning gained
A glimpse of Paradise.

His voice was rich and deep and his eyes lingered on hers, causing the poet's words to seem his own. And he effectively rendered her speechless for what seemed like the zillionth time in just the short while they'd been together.

"Did I get it right?"

"Yes!" The word burst out of her stunned mouth. *Get a grip on yourself and say something intelligent before he starts thinking he's talking to a prematurely aged teenager.* "Yes, you did," she said in a more grown-up voice. "That's 'If It Be Sin' by DeMass, isn't it? Are you a poetry fan?"

Laughing, he took her hand and planted a quick, playful kiss on it.

"What I am is a man with a pretty good memory who had one hell of a hard sophomore English teacher who terrified him and pounded poetry into his head so thoroughly that more than a decade later it's still stuck there."

"Oh, God. I did that to you?"

"Yes, Ms. Cox, you certainly did."

Unexpectedly, Candice blushed. "What grade did I give you?"

"A 'C,' and I was grateful for it. And I do believe you might have also given me an ulcer as well as several painful hard-ons that semester, too." He laughed. Then, before she could sputter a reply about the C, the ulcer or (embarrassingly) the hard-ons, he glanced around them. "Isn't this your place?"

Surprised, Candice realized that they were standing in her driveway. "Yes, it is." She smiled at him and had to press her palms against her legs to stop her hands from fidgeting. "Thanks for walking me home."

"Entirely my pleasure." He studied her for a moment, and his charming smile faltered as his expression grew more serious. "I'd—I'd like to see you again," he said quickly, then held up his hand to cut her off when she automatically opened her mouth to tell him no. "Wait. Before you shoot me down I'd like you to answer one question for me. Did you enjoy talking to me?"

"Yes." The answer came easily.

"Because I'm an ex-student or because you think I'm a man who is interesting and maybe slightly charming?"

"That's two questions," she said.

"Nope—it's the same question, just with two parts. Kinda like some of those hellish essay questions you used to torture us with."

She smiled begrudgingly at him, and decided to tell him the truth. "Because I find you interesting."

"And maybe a little charming?"

"Maybe . . ."

"Then why not agree to see me again?"

"Justin, I'm forty."

He waited, looking at her as if there had to be more to it than that.

She sighed. "Justin," she tried again, "I'm forty years old and you're—"

"Yes, I know. I got a C in English, but I did better in math. You're fourteen years older than I am. You're also smart and funny and easy to talk to and very, very sexy. Seriously, Candice. Try finding all those qualities in girls half your age. It's next to impossible." When she looked like she wanted to argue with him, he took her hand and said, "Okay, if our age difference bothers you that much, how about let's not call it a real date? Let's call it . . . an exercise appointment."

"An exercise appointment?"

"You jog every day, don't you?"

"Almost."

"Will you be jogging tomorrow?"

"Probably."

"Then how about we make an appointment to jog together tomorrow?"

"Okay," she heard herself say. "I'll jog by Wolf Creek at about sevenish."

"You're awesome! See you tomorrow." He shot her a blazing smile, kicked into a youthful, athletic jog, and disappeared into the fading light of dusk around the curve in the road.

Awesome? She cringed. *Like, wow. I am, like, totally awesome.*

Laughing softly at her own silliness, she skipped lightly up the stairs into her house. Refusing to berate herself for being a horny middle-aged letch, Candice poured herself a cold glass of water. She had the whole day tomorrow to consider if she really was going to show up for their "appointment" or not. She wouldn't think about it now. And anyway, her eye caught sight of the notebook and pencil sitting on her desk where she'd left them. She had homework to do.

Candice grinned.

She also had lines of poetry unexpectedly popping into her mind. Godiva had been partially right. Being in the presence of a werewolf had certainly unblocked her—even if an evening of conversation hadn't been exactly what her witchy friend had been recommending. Eagerly, she sat down and put pencil to the unfinished page, taking up easily where she'd left off.

You ask, what now?
Well, love comes with the night,
in the most inexplicable places
leaving the most unexplainable traces.

Candice giggled, and kept writing.

You see ... a wolfman is the man for me!

Hmm . . . maybe she would meet Justin tomorrow.

✳ 4 ✳

He thought about her a lot more than he'd intended to. He was supposed to show up at a keg party in the forest—rumor had it that several of the not-so-innocent high school seniors from the cheerleading squad were curious about just how well werewolves could use their tongues . . . not an invitation he had declined in the past. But tonight it felt, well, *wrong* to be rolling around the forest with girls Candice had probably taught in English class— and not a decade or so ago.

Actually, if he was being really honest with himself, his life had begun to wear on him. Or, more accurately, to bore him. He hated the restaurant. His older brothers were already firmly ensconced in management positions—hence the fact that he had been relegated to making purchasing runs for them. Not that anyone expected more of him. He'd always been "that Justin—so incorrigible and handsome!" He'd never been taken seriously. But, then again, it hadn't really mattered to him. He'd always been into having fun . . . feeling good.

When had that started to change?

He wasn't really sure. But he knew he hadn't been giving Candice a slick line tonight when he'd told her that she was smart and funny and sexy. Very, very sexy. And that he hadn't found that combination of qualities in twenty-something girls. She challenged him. She made him think. And she turned him on. He'd had no idea what a lethal mixture those things were before he spent an evening in Ms. Cox's stimulating company. He wanted to see her again. Badly. More than that, he wanted her to want him. If a woman like that could want him . . . what couldn't a man accomplish if he won the love of a woman like that?

So tonight, instead of joining the orgy in the woods he was much more interested in searching the back of his closet for an old textbook from a freshman lit class he'd taken before dropping out of the Denver Art Institute. Funny . . . he hadn't thought about his failed attempt at an art major in years. But those eyes of hers. They'd made him remember. They were mossy green—a color that cried to be painted.

Those eyes . . .

Justin grabbed the literature book and then flipped open his laptop. A few simple clicks took him to the website of Mysteria High School—Home of the Fighting Fairies. He smiled triumphantly. Sure enough, there was a complete list of faculty phone numbers.

Candice jumped when her cell phone made the little three-tone sound it did when she had a text message. She wiped her eyes, stuck her reading glasses on top of her head, and reluctantly took her nose out of Tanith Lee's *Silver Metal Lover*.

"Why do you insist on reading and rereading this book? You know what happens, and you know it makes you cry. You," she told herself sternly before blowing her nose, "are a ridiculous romantic. And you're old enough to know better." She sighed. Ridiculous or not, she truly loved the story of a robot finding his soul through loving a woman. Not that it could really happen. Even putting aside the fact that it wasn't possible to make humanlike robots, it was an impossible dream that a man could really become . . . well . . . *more* simply through the love of an exceptional woman. After all, she was exceptional (wasn't she?) and she had the unquestionable proof of ex-husbands one through five being total turds—despite her loving attempts.

Of course, a little voice whispered through her conscience, maybe she hadn't really loved any of them . . . maybe true love *did* have the power to create souls and make miracles.

"Please," she scoffed aloud at herself, "grow the fuck up."

Then, remembering what had interrupted her, Candice reached for her phone. Flipping it open she keyed up the one new text message.

Looking forward to our "appointment" tomorrow @ 7:00. J
P.S. you have beautiful eyes

She felt a rush of sweet excitement—a heady, intoxicating feeling she hadn't experienced in years. No matter how *ridiculous,* she had a date with a twenty-six-and-a-half-year-old man.

It took forever for it to be evening. Candice had chosen, vetoed, and rechosen what she was going to wear. Then she'd cursed herself over and over. Why the hell hadn't she agreed to a normal date? One where she could drive up in her chic Mini and meet him at a nice restaurant somewhere out of town. (Way out of town.) She'd have chosen her sexy little black dress that displayed all of her assets and hid most of her imperfections. Her makeup would have been meticulously applied. And her hair would have been Truly Big and Ready for Flirtatious Flinging About. She could have dazzled him with her experience and good taste in choosing excellent wine, and then ordered from any menu with the confidence and flair that can only be earned through maturity and experience. She, in short, would have had the upper hand.

Instead she was trying to figure out which of her rather old sports bras was the least tattered, and which cotton panties weren't totally grandma-ish. As if there was such a thing as an un-grandma-ish cotton workout panty. Why, oh why hadn't she bought new sports bras at the last Victoria's Secret sale? Oh yeah, she remembered . . . *they don't have real, usable sports bras at Victoria's Secret!*

Oh, God. Would he see her bra and panties? Just the thought made her feel like she wanted to puke her guts up.

No! Of course he wouldn't see her panties! She was meeting him for a quick jog, not a quick fuck.

Regardless, somehow she found herself in the bathroom. Naked. Staring through her fingers into the full-length mirror at her body as if she was watching a horror flick.

Looking at myself totally naked and under fluorescent lights just can't be healthy. But she continued to stare and criticize.

Sure, she wasn't awful looking. Candice forced the shielding fingers from her eyes. Okay. She wasn't really that bad. She'd been thinner and tighter, but her skin was soft and smooth, and she was definitely curvy. Maybe even lush. She shook her head, as if to clear the bizarre notions from it. "Lush" and "curvy" were not "young" and "tight-assed." There was just no way she was going to get naked in front of and have sex with a twenty-six-and-a-half-year-old. No. Fucking. Way.

Maybe he wouldn't be there. He probably wouldn't be there. Why would he want to be there? He could have just been being polite yesterday. He probably was just being nice. She had misinterpreted. He hadn't really flirted and come on to her. It was silly, really. He was so damn young. Sure, she was attractive, but please. She was almost fifteen years older. No way was he *interested* in her. Not like *that*.

"Hey there, beautiful."

She'd told herself that she was ready to see him—or ready for him to stand her up. Either was fine. Really. Whatever. Who cared? But then he was there, calling her beautiful and smiling his sexy, boy/man smile, and she felt the same dizzying rush of excitement she'd felt when he'd sent her the message the night before. And, dear sweet Lord, he was even more handsome than she'd remembered. Had she been blocking? Was it temporary amnesia? How could she not have been obsessing all day over his height and the incredible width of those shoulders, and that amazing jawline. . . .

"Hi," she said breathlessly, glad that she'd agreed to meet him at the creek so that she had an excuse other than just the sight of him to be breathing hard.

"How do you feel about trying something new today?"

His flirty smile made her stomach tighten. Oh, God, if only he knew.

Never mind. It was probably best that he didn't know.

Be normal! Talk to him!

"What do you have in mind?"

His eyes sparkled as he jerked his head, pointing his chin away from the road and into the forest. Then, with a confident, deep voice he recited, "'I shall be telling this with a sigh somewhere ages and ages hence: Two roads diverged in a wood, and I—I took the one less traveled by.'"

He was actually quoting poetry to her. Again. Her cheeks felt warmed by more than the short jog through the graveyard. "A little Robert Frost?"

"A very little, I'm afraid. And don't be too impressed. I freely admit to memorizing it this afternoon."

"You know, I don't remember you being this interested in poetry in high school."

"Would it help if I made my voice crack and stared, slack-jawed, at your boobs?"

"Only if your intention is to scare me out of the forest."

His smile was intimate. "That is not my intention."

She almost asked what his intentions were . . . but she didn't want to know. What if he gave her a blank look and said, "I thought we'd be friends"? She'd fucking die. But whether it'd be from relief or disappointment, she wasn't sure. She only realized that she'd been standing there silently staring at him when his smile faded and his tone became more serious.

"Candice, if you don't want to go off into the woods with me, all you have to do is say the word. I'll understand. I just thought that you might like exploring a hiking path I know about. That way we could get our exercise and still be able to talk. I don't know about you, but I've never mastered the talent of jogging and talking at the same time."

She met his eyes. His gaze was open and honest—vulnerable, even. Could he be as nervous as she felt? And then came the startling revelation—he had to be *more* nervous. She was almost fifteen years his senior and his ex-teacher. She was more experienced and more confident. She could reject him with a neatly turned phrase and a patronizing, disdainful look. She definitely had the high ground, even if she wasn't perfectly coiffed and perched on a posh chair at an elegant restaurant. Disregarding the rather ridiculous question of whether or not this was a real date, Justin had put himself in a position where he could be thoroughly humiliated and ultimately rejected by her, yet here he was, with a sweet smile on his handsome face, looking for all the world like a man who was doing his best to woo a woman.

"Do you remember the rest of the quote?" she asked, smiling softly at him.

"The Frost quote? No—I just memorized that far." His cheeks flushed a little with the admission.

"Frost concluded it, 'I took the one less traveled by, and that has made all the difference.' How about we take your path—the one less traveled by?"

Refreshingly, he didn't attempt to hide his relief with a suave turn of phrase or a knowing look. Instead he just smiled and said, "I promise that it will make all the difference."

Justin took her hand and led her into the forest.

☀ 5 ☀

"All this time I've been jogging by the creek, and I had no idea a hiking path like this was so close."

"That's one good thing about being a werewolf. I have definitely gotten to know these woods."

He'd spoken nonchalantly, but she could feel his look and the expectant silence that screamed, "I'm waiting for you to freak out because I'm a wolf!" So she didn't respond right away. Instead she picked her way carefully over a large log that had fallen across the trail.

"You're right. Knowing the secret paths in the woods is one

good thing about being a werewolf. What's another?" she asked, matching his nonchalant tone.

He hesitated only a moment. "The physical power."

"You mean when you're in your wolf form?"

Justin slowed down and studied her face. "Do you really want to know, or are you just making polite conversation?"

"I'm intrigued," she said honestly.

"There's physical power in both forms, and in both I can tap into the magic in these hills pretty easily. In this form I'm stronger than a human man. And not just physically. My senses are more acute. My memory is better." He grinned a little sheepishly. "I guess that means I should have made better than a C in your class."

"Nah," she said. "You weren't a man then. You probably hadn't attained all of your"—she paused and made a vague, fluttery gesture at him with her hand—"uh, Spidey senses yet."

His infectious laugh rolled around them. "Spidey senses? On a werewolf? Are you thinking I might be a hairy Peter Parker?"

"Oh, God, no!" she said with mock horror. "If I was going to fantasize about walking through the woods with a superhero it wouldn't be one that was really just a dorky kid. Let's try Bruce Wayne, shall we?"

"How about a happy medium? How about walking through the woods with a grown-up superhero who is modestly employed—I don't exactly have Batman's resources." The trail took a sharp upward turn and Justin stopped, pulling her gently back to his side when she started to climb ahead of him. "Want to test my superhuman powers?"

She narrowed her eyes at him. "Does this involve either: one, me being unattractively carried away by any type of a creature who has more than two arms, or two, your having the ability to see through any article of my clothing?"

He rubbed his chin, considering. "No and no."

"Then fine. I agree to the test."

"Okay. You have to hold totally still."

He walked a tight circle around her and Candice instantly noticed the difference in the way he moved. His body language was once again that of the man who had entered the clearing the day before—the warrior god who had not known who she was. He positioned himself behind her, standing so close that she could feel him draw in a deep breath. Then he bent, and whispered huskily into her ear.

"You don't wear real perfume."

She started to turn to answer him, but his words, which were spoken hot against her neck, stopped her.

"You must hold totally still."

She froze, whispering back. "What do you mean by not real perfume?"

"You don't buy that packaged and bottled stuff other women like so much and spray too much of on their bodies. Not you. Instead, you put drops of pure lavender oil behind your ears, on your wrists"—he drew another breath, then exhaled the warmth of his words against her neck—"and between your breasts. Am I right?"

"Yes, you're right."

Slowly, his hand rose to lightly, lightly caress her hair before he gently fisted it and pressed his face into it, taking a deep, hot breath. She focused on not trembling, and thought how glad she was that she'd conveniently "forgotten" to pull it up in a ponytail.

"You never blow-dry your hair. You let the air dry it. And you prefer the night air to the warmer, daylight breeze."

This time she was truly amazed. How the hell could he know that?

"Am I right?" he asked again.

"Yes," she whispered. "How did you know?"

"Your hair smells like moonlight and shadows, and I know those scents intimately." His hands were still in her hair. "Why do you prefer the night air?"

"It's something that started when I was a little girl. In the summer I'd wash my hair at night and then sit on the porch with a flashlight and read. My dad used to laugh and say that the moonlight made my hair wavy like the tide. I guess it's a habit that stuck."

"I'm glad. I like moon wavy hair," he said.

"Do you?"

Justin gently nuzzled the ear he was whispering into. "Yes."

His breath sent chills down her body that lodged in her thighs, making her legs feel wobbly and semidrunk. She was relieved when he took his mouth from her ear and moved back around in front of her. Smiling, he was once more just a handsome young man.

"Impressed by my superpowers?"

"Very."

"Good. You'll love my next display of EWP."

"EWP?"

"Extrawerewolfory perception," he said, with only a slight glint in his eyes. "So. Are you hungry?"

"If I say yes are you going to grow fur and chase down some poor helpless rabbit?"

"Maybe another time. Right now if you said you were hungry I'd simply clap my hands twice and then help you climb up the rise in the path so I could show you that I made your wish come true."

"Okay, I'll bite. I'm hungry."

He waggled his eyebrows and leered at her. "Be careful, Ms. Cox—mine is the species that bites."

Before she could respond with the pithy reply she was formulating, he grabbed her hand and pulled her up the incline. Candice glanced around, surprised that the dense woods had suddenly given way to a lovely meadow of soft grass that was dotted with blue wildflowers. Fireflies flitted in the dim evening light, looking like miniature fairies. (Candice squinted her eyes and made certain that they weren't actually fairies. God, she hated fairies.) And then her surprise doubled. Not far from the path someone had spread a large plaid blanket, on which sat a huge wicker picnic basket and a bucket filled with ice and a bottle of white wine.

"You see what happens when you date a superhero?" he said.

"This isn't a date. It's an appointment," she said automatically.

"Well, I think that depends."

"On what?"

"On the good-night kiss."

Smiling, he led her over to the picnic dinner he had so meticulously chosen, packed, and then brought out into the forest just for her.

* 6 *

The dinner was scrumptious. Candice was amazed by the obvious care he'd taken with everything. From the excellent dry white wine from Venice and the real crystal goblets he served it in, to the decadently tender prime rib sandwiches and fresh fruit—everything was better than perfect. And that included the conversation. She couldn't believe how easy he was to talk to. He was actually smart! A closet history buff, he told her stories about the settlers who had founded the various cities in Colorado—something she knew little about because she'd always focused on European instead of American lit.

And he noticed everything. Not just the details of the meal, but he noticed when the inflection of her voice changed, when she was distracted by the beauty of the blue wildflowers (which he promptly picked for her), and when she talked about her new passion—finishing her master's and moving to Denver. He discussed the aspects of her new future animatedly. Unlike Godiva, he didn't try to talk her into staying or dissuade her from following her dream. Justin honestly seemed to understand her need to move on.

But what surprised Candice most was how easy it was for her to forget he was so young. She wasn't sure when it happened—somewhere between their discussion of the stupidity of the underfunded state education initiatives, and their mutual (and, on her part, rather blasphemous) agreement that the *Lord of the Rings* movies were actually better than the books—but Candice Cox totally stopped thinking of him as ohmygodhe'ssofuckingyoung Justin, and started seeing him as the man she was out on a date with.

"So, how's the poetry assignment coming?" he asked.

"Better, I think. At least I got a little written last night." She sipped her wine. Maybe it was the third glass of wine, or the intimate silence that surrounded them, but it felt easy for her to speak half-formed dreams aloud. "You know what's weird? I'm doing this whole master's thing so I can get a job reading other people's writing, but I think I'm finding out that I actually like doing the writing part myself."

"You want to write a book?"

"I don't know. Maybe. Right now all I know is that I'd like to write something that—" she broke off, suddenly embarrassed.

"That what?" he prompted.

She met his amber gaze. He was so sincere. Rarely had she known a man who listened as well as he did. There was something about the way he looked at her, and spoke to her—as if he thought she was interesting and smart and he honestly cared about what she had to say.

It was more intoxicating than the Venetian wine.

"I'd like to write something that would have the ability to make people feel. It could be a book, or short stories, or maybe even poetry. What it is isn't important. What is important is that what I write evokes feelings in those who read it."

His gaze was hot and intense on hers as Justin leaned toward her, resting his hand on her knee. "I know exactly what you mean. That's how I always felt about my art. I didn't care if I was painting or sculpting or just sketching with plain charcoal. I wanted people to feel what I felt."

"Why did you stop, Justin?" she asked softly.

"I don't really know. . . ." His eyes dropped from hers. "One day I was a college freshman at the Art Institute—the next I'd washed out. I'm pretty sure it had something to do with me changing my major from art to beer and women." His lips twisted in self-mockery. "A double major actually. I made stupid choices—a string of stupid choices—and then I was back in Mysteria working at the restaurant."

She wanted to tell him that it wasn't too late for him to go to college, that he could get a portfolio together and get back into the Art Institute, but she hesitated. Did he really need her to turn into a teacher and lecture him? She didn't think so, and she also didn't want to. She liked being his date and not his mentor. Candice put her hand on top of his.

"Sometimes it's easy to get lost. You let your art get lost when you dropped out of college. I let good sense get lost when I committed serial matrimony. I suppose all either of us can do is to learn from our mistakes."

"I'm glad you're divorced." He smiled and added, "Again."

"Well, I'm with you on that one."

"Do you mind if I ask why none of your marriages worked?"

"I don't mind you asking, but I'm not sure I have an answer for you, even though I should because the ending of each of them felt the same—so you'd think I'd learn how to define the problem, if not fix it." She sighed. "I stopped loving them. Each one. Actually, it's more accurate to say that I stopped liking each of them first, *then* I couldn't love them anymore. They were five different kinds of men, and, as much as I kid around about it, none of them were bad men. I wouldn't have married a bad man. Still, it didn't work out with any of them, which, naturally, points to the one common denominator—me." She glanced up at him. He was watching her intently, and not in that patronizing "I'll just let the woman talk so I can get into her panties" kind of way. His amber eyes were interested—his expression plainly said he was involved in what she was saying. Candice drew a deep breath. "I'll tell you something I've never told anyone. I think I fail at relationships because I don't have any magic."

His brow wrinkled. "But most places aren't like Mysteria. Outside of here lots of people don't have magic and they manage to have happy marriages."

"Nope. I don't think so. I don't think you have to live in totally bizarre Mysteria to have magic. See, I think the ability to have a successful, happy marriage is a special kind of magic, and that special magic exists all over the world. The problem with me is that I'm doomed because I have nonmagic, just like I have nonmarriages and nonrelationships."

"Maybe"—he reached up and cupped the side of her cheek with his hand—"you just need to quit trying so hard."

Then, amazingly, Justin leaned forward and kissed her. It was a gentle kiss, not accompanied by any intrusive thrustings of tongue and teeth. She'd worried about that when she'd allowed herself to think about kissing him. Would a twenty-something be a bully kisser? Would he blindly stick his mouth on hers and proceed to grind any and all available body parts against her? It'd been too damn long since she'd kissed a man this young—she couldn't remember how they did it. But she needn't have worried. The boy/man/wolf kissed like a dream . . .

a deliciously erotic dream. His mouth was a warm caress against hers—not a demand, but a seductive question.

"You taste like lavender and wine," he murmured, his lips lingering near hers.

"You taste like sex," she whispered back before her better sense could stop the words. "Erotic and decadent, and very, very male."

He chuckled and his lips moved to her neck. "That's because I'm still using my superpowers on you." His tongue flicked out to tease the gentle slope of smooth flesh where her neck met her shoulder. "But maybe you don't believe me. Maybe you need more proof first."

"If I say I do, does that mean you won't stop?" she said breathlessly.

"I won't stop unless you tell me to."

"Then we may be here all night," she moaned.

He pressed her down into the blanket and slid his hand under her T-shirt. "I'm good with all night."

She let her hands travel up his arms to his chest. God, his body was hard! And more than just between his legs (although it was already decidedly obvious that he didn't suffer from the same unfortunate and very flaccid problem her last ex-husband had). Utterly fascinated, she tugged at his shirt until he took his hands from her long enough to pull it over his head.

Dear sweet Lord—she'd died and, despite her numerous sins and bad language, gone straight to heaven. He looked better unclothed—and that was one hell of a compliment because he had looked scrumptious with his shirt on. He was truly a beautiful man.

Then his hands were tugging up her shirt. She started to help him . . . and remembered: 1) that she was wearing her least stretched out and frayed sports bra—"least" in no way meaning that it was attractive, and 2) she was forty. Suddenly he was, once again, ohmygodhe'ssofuckingyoung Justin.

"Uh, wait. I'm—I'm not completely okay with this," she said quickly, smoothing down her shirt while she avoided meeting his eyes.

Instantly, he stopped. But he didn't pull away from her. Nor did he throw a fit because he had a hard-on and needed to have sex now. He just shifted his weight so that she was resting comfortably in his arms. Then he lifted her chin with his finger, gently making her meet his gaze.

"Did I do something wrong?" he asked.

"No. It's not you."

He cocked an eyebrow at her and smiled crookedly. "Is there someone else here I don't know about?"

"Of course not."

"Then is it that you don't want me?"

"Of course not!"

"Candice, I'm going to be honest with you. For the past several years I haven't been connected to much—not another person or a job or even a place. I've been playing at life and just letting time pass. But with you I feel a connection, and that's something I'm not used to. I want to see where it takes us. If that means going slow physically, I will. But I have to tell you that the truth is I want you more than I've ever wanted any woman in my life."

His amber eyes had darkened to the color of aged Scotch. She could feel the sexual tension in his body. She loved the intensity with which he looked at her, and the way his hands lingered on hers. And she knew if she didn't make love to this beautiful young man that she would regret it forever.

Deliberately, she sat up and, keeping her eyes fixed on his, she pulled off her shirt. Then she reached behind her and undid her sports bra, shrugging it off her shoulders. The late evening air was cool against the heat of her skin, and her nipples puckered. Justin's gaze dropped from her eyes to her naked breasts. He reached forward and took her heavy breasts in his hands, lifting and caressing them.

"God, you're beautiful," he said huskily. "Look at you! You're not some plastic girl who hasn't lived enough to know there are sexier things than fake boobs and lace bras that match their thongs that match the color they paint their toes." He bent and kissed the swell of her breast, then let his tongue tease her already aroused nipple while she moaned and arched into him. "You're an earth goddess, rich and ripe and desirable."

He pressed her back into the blanket again, his lips and tongue teasing her breasts. His mouth moved slowly down her stomach, kissing the waist of her shorts. Before she could begin to get nervous about the fact that her stomach wasn't as flat as it had been ten years before, she heard him murmur, "Your skin is like silk, and you taste like lavender-scented honey."

She probably would have let him pull off her shorts then, but he slid down, until he knelt at her feet. Smiling at her, he took off her running shoes and socks. When he kissed the arch of her foot she had a moment to think about how desperately glad she was that she'd had a pedicure just two days ago, then he moved from her foot to her calf, kneading it much as he had done the day before. Only now he interspersed his caresses with soft kisses as he made his way slowly up her leg.

"Justin . . ." His name was a moan, and all thoughts of statutory rape and moral turpitude permanently flew from her mind.

"Sssh," he breathed against the sensitive spot behind her knee. "Let me worship you like the goddess you are, and allow me to teach you what I've learned since I left your class."

"A little role reversal?" she asked breathlessly, making no move to stop him as his lips grazed her inner thigh.

"Absolutely, Ms. Cox. It's time you quit worrying about marriages and relationships and nonmagic and just relax and enjoy a man who appreciates what an exceptional woman you are and can make you feel as good as you deserve to feel." He nuzzled the leg of her shorts up so that when he spoke his mouth moved, hot and insistent, against the very top of her inner thigh. "What I've learned is how to use my tongue and mouth to bring a woman to orgasm before I fill her body with mine and stroke her into another climax and then another."

"Do you do this often?" The thought of the possibility that she might be just another in a long line of female conquests began to dissipate her horny haze.

"No," he moaned, his mouth on her skin. "Don't think that. It's you I want to taste—you I want to pleasure. I've fantasized about you for years. You have no idea how much I want you and how special you are to me. Let me make my fantasies real. Let me taste you."

When he pulled at the waist of her shorts, she willingly lifted to make his job easier. As she settled back against the blanket, her eyes were drawn over his shoulder to the darkening sky and she felt a little jolt as she realized how close it was to sunset . . . which would be followed by moonrise . . . and a nearly full moon rise at that.

Observant as ever, Justin read the new tension in her body. He saw her eyes fixed on the sky and the clear concern in her face.

"I promise that you have nothing to fear from me."

Reluctantly, her gaze left the sky and met his eyes. "But when the full moon rises, you're a wolf, aren't you?"

"Actually, there's always a little of the wolf in me, full moon or not," he said, nipping her stomach gently and then lowering his head to taste her with a long lick of his tongue.

Her breath caught in surprise and she had to bite her lip to stifle a breathy moan.

He kissed her thigh and then smiled up at her. "Remember, your magic is nonmagic. Which means I am unable to shift my shape around you. I am in man form right now, and as long as I'm close to you I'll stay in that form." He nuzzled her thigh and kissed her again. "Let me make love to you, my sweet Candy." His voice caressed her name. "Let me be your lover."

"I know exactly what you need . . . a werewolf lover." Godiva's voice whispered through her mind. Maybe her friend was right. And why not? Justin appreciated her. He listened to her and made her feel beautiful and desirable. What was wrong with her taking a young, virile lover who wanted to worship her like a goddess? . . .

With a triumphant smile, she made her decision.

"If you can't change form as long as I'm close to you, I guess the right answer is for me to keep you *very* close to me." She pulled the young werewolf to her and let his victorious growl vibrate against her naked skin.

Justin had been right. He had learned a hell of a lot since he'd left her classroom. And his tongue . . . not only did he use it between her legs with such enthusiasm that her vibrator would forever after seem a weak substitute, but his ability to listen (amazingly enough) hadn't stopped when his dick hardened. He listened and responded when she showed him the secret place low on her stomach that was so ultrasensitive. He paid attention to that spot at the base of her neck. And his kisses . . . his kisses were an erotic adventure.

When he'd brought her to climax three times he finally moaned that he couldn't wait anymore, and she'd reveled in the hard length of him as she guided him within her slick, ready folds. He'd tried to hold back—tried not to be too rough. She'd bit him on the shoulder and told him fiercely that she wasn't a breakable young girl—that she wanted him—all of him. His growl had been sensual music. She gripped his hard hips with her legs and met his thrusts with equal strength, urging him on until he cried her name and spent himself within her.

* 7 *

Godiva had known what she was talking about. Having a were-wolf lover was *spectacular*. Especially such a young werewolf lover. God, she'd almost forgotten the incredibly sexy strength of a young man's body. And recovery time! Jeesh. That *boy* had been better than a recharged vibrator. Way better. She was so glad it was the weekend and there was no school the next day. They'd made love for hours, and he was still nibbling at her neck when he'd walked her home. She jumped the steps into her house two at a time. He made her feel twenty again. No! She took that back. She didn't feel twenty again—no way did she want to feel that stupid and unconfident again. Justin made her feel fabulous and forty, which was exactly what she was.

Candice had taken a long bath, delighted with the unaccustomed soreness of her body. And then, replete, she'd slept till noon. Noon! And only woke up then because her cell phone had toned at her, telling her she had a text message. She flipped it open, feeling a rush of pleasure even before she saw the text.

Are you busy tonight? I have a surprise for you.

What was he up to now? She grinned and replied:

More spidey sense?

His reply was a single word.

Better

She laughed out loud. This was fun! And, no. She wasn't going to go on and on with herself about how long it'd been since she'd had this kind of fun . . . and that she might be having *too* much fun *too* soon. No. She was just going to enjoy herself.

I think I can fit you into my schedule.

P. C. CAST

She waited impatiently for the tone that signaled his reply, and when it came it sounded like beautiful music—even though she was completely aware of how ridiculously romantic that seemed.

Be on your deck at dusk. And be ready . . .

Be on her deck at dusk? And be ready for what? But she forced herself not to text him back and ask for details. She wanted to break her old habits. She overanalyzed things ("things" being defined as "men"). She knew she did it, and she knew she had gotten worse as she'd gotten older.

"Not this time," she muttered as she fixed herself a cup of her favorite green tea and stuck a couple pieces of toast in the toaster. "This time is going to be different. This time I'm not looking for a husband; I'm looking for fun."

Candice took her tea, toast, a pencil, and the pad of paper she'd started writing her poem on the day before out onto the wonderful wood deck that wrapped the length of the back of her house and looked out into the woods that surrounded Mysteria. She curled up cross-legged on the comfortable wicker rocker that sat beside the little wicker table.

It was such a beautiful day! The woods, always magical (literally and figuratively) looked like a romantic dream come to life. All that it lacked was the knight and the white horse and . . .

Good lord! What was happening to her? She was making her own self sick.

"Snap out of it and get to writing so you can get to the good stuff tonight." Then, humming "Tonight, Tonight" from *West Side Story* she looked at the partially written poem.

> *Keep your Errol Flynns, Paul Newmans, Mel Gibsons*
> *all puppets—empty masquerades.*
> *Tom, Dick, and Harry, too*
> *the boy next door*
> *I want no more.*
> *You ask, what now?*
> *Well, love comes with the night,*
> *in the most inexplicable places*
> *leaving the most unexplainable traces.*
> *You see . . . a wolfman is the man for me!*

She smiled and began to write from there.

> *True, hair in the sink is copious,*

Two hours later she should have been frustrated and annoyed. She was, after all, staring at the same line she'd written earlier and nothing else was coming. Well, not exactly nothing. She'd written line after line after line, but nothing seemed to work. Nothing could begin to capture the new, crystal bright feeling of happiness and expectation that was building inside of her, and that was the feeling she wanted her poem to evoke.

"Ah, hell! Never mind. I'll write it tomorrow." She had a date to get ready for, a really hot date at that, which called for eyebrow plucking, leg shaving, a full pedicure and manicure, and lots of hair primping. Not to mention that she was going to dig through some of the boxes she'd moved into the basement to find what she'd done with her really sexy lingerie.

"Tonight I will not be wearing a sports bra and grandma panties," she promised the air around her. Had she not been so busy trying (unsuccessfully) not to giggle like a girl, she would have noticed the gaggle of pink-winged fairies who, overhearing her, had taken off in a burst of silver glitter and musical laughter out over the trees, heading in the direction of their favorite witch's house.

Justin wanted to do something special for her. He'd been up most of the night thinking about what he could do—and about her. Her skin and her body . . . he'd never felt anything as lush and inviting. So this was what it was like to be with a woman versus a girl! Twenty-somethings paled in comparison to Candice. And he could talk to her! He'd actually talked with her about dreams he'd thought were long dead. He couldn't remember the last time he'd even thought about painting, yet here he was, heading to her place with the huge book he'd checked out from the library, one with glossy, full-color pictures of famous pieces of art, tucked under his arm. With his other arm he carried a bag filled with several cuts of prime fillet steaks from his family's restaurant, each broiled and spiced to perfection, and one of the brightly checked tablecloths they used in the dining room. He smiled as he got closer to her house and left the road to circle around to her backyard. When he could peer through the thick trees and just barely make out her deck, he put the book and the bag down, spread the tablecloth out over the leafy ground, and opened the boxes, letting the aroma of expensive steak waft in the light evening breeze.

He didn't have long to wait. He heard their giggles and the whirring of their wings before he saw them. Then, poof! He was standing in the center of a cloud of fairies who, as soon as they spotted the steaks, squealed with pleasure and began a dive-bomb-like descent.

"Wait!" He growled menacingly and stood protectively over the delectable meal. The fairies paused, midswoop. "If you want the steaks you have to do something for me."

Four of the glittering miniature nymphs glided toward him. They were only about as big as an outstretched hand, but their beauty was not diminished by size. They smiled coquettishly at him.

"We know you, wolfman," the four trilled together, magically harmonizing. "We've often watched you pleasure females in the forest." They ran their hands suggestively down their naked bodies. "We would be happy to do *something* for you."

He quickly put his hands up, as if fending off an attack. "No, no, no. You don't understand. The favor I need is not quite so personal."

"What a shame." They pouted prettily.

"Do you want the steaks or not?" He already knew their answer. Fairies craved red meat, but they never got enough. They could really be a pain in the ass; they were almost as bad as termites or fleas. His dad had to spray the restaurant for them monthly.

"We want the meat!" the entire group answered together.

"Good. Then this is all I need you to do." He picked up the thick art book and then hesitated before he opened it to one of the three pages he'd marked earlier. "Do you know the teacher who lives in the cabin right there?" He pointed through the trees at Candice's house.

As a group the fairies nodded.

"You know what she looks like?"

They nodded again, causing their long, shining hair to sparkle and glisten and float around them like slightly tarnished, then glittered, haloes.

"Excellent. Here's what I need you to do . . ." Justin opened the book. The fairies flocked around him, making curious little cooing noises as he gave them their orders.

Candice was going to be totally surprised!

* * *

Candice was sitting in her wicker chair sipping an excellent glass of chilled chardonnay when he stepped out of the forest and onto the grass of her backyard. There was just enough light left in the dusky sky to see that his smile was reflected by the sparkle in his amber eyes.

"Hello, Ms. Cox," he said mischievously.

"Hello, Justin," she said in her best teacher voice. "Did you stop by for a little detention?"

"I don't know." His grin widened. "I think I've been a pretty good boy lately."

"Yes, you certainly have," she said, feeling suddenly very warm.

"Not that I wouldn't like being locked in a room alone with you."

"So my surprise has to do with locks?"

"No, Miss Impatient. Nothing like that." He climbed the deck stairs and leaned down to kiss her lightly. "You look beautiful tonight. Love the short skirt."

Candice didn't think she'd ever been so grateful for having good legs.

"Thank you. Wine?" she offered.

"I'd love some, thanks."

She poured him a glass of sun-colored wine. Just before he

sat in the empty wicker chair across from her he looked out toward the forest, raised his hand, and yelled, "Action!"

Instantly, the sky over the trees began to glitter like Fourth of July sparklers, and the breeze carried the sound of silly feminine laughter to them.

Candice scowled. "Fairies. What are they up to?"

"Keep watching," Justin said, sipping his wine.

"I do not like fairies," she grumbled. Still frowning, she looked back at the sparkling sky and gasped. A picture was forming from the glistening fairy dust.

"Oh, my God! It's the *Mona Lisa*!"

"Keep watching," Justin repeated.

Mona Lisa's face changed. Candice's mouth fell open. "It's me!"

Justin laughed and lifted her hand from where it rested on the little table. He kissed her palm. "Yep, it is."

Candice was still staring at the glowing portrait when the picture shifted and changed. Now she was looking at a hauntingly beautiful woman with long red hair who was sitting in a small boat.

"Waterhouse's *Lady of Shalott*!" Then it, too, changed and she was watching herself frozen in time as the lady who was cursed to sing her last song as she floated down to Camelot.

Entranced, she watched the picture dissipate and begin to form again as another famous woman. This time it wasn't a painting the fairies were reproducing. It was the eternally graceful statue of the winged Nike. And then, as if the Greek gods had ordered a miracle, Candice's face and neck, even her long blonde hair, appeared to complete the glorious statue. Candice laughed and clapped her hands.

Justin hardly glanced at the fairy artwork. He couldn't stop looking at Candice. Uninhibited joy had transformed her face from pretty to stunning. Everything inside him screamed, *Her! She's the one I'm meant to be with!*

Candice gasped again as the new painting took form. "This is one of my all-time favorites! *Meeting on Turret Stairs* by Burton." She made a happy little cry. "Justin! It's us!"

Then he did pull his eyes from her to look at the sky. Sure enough, the incredibly romantic scene of the knight passing his lady on the narrow stairway had been altered so that it was the two of them. The knight was kissing his lady's arm as she leaned dramatically against the stone wall of the castle; both of them were clearly overwhelmed by a desire so real it seemed to leap off the painting and become tangible. He hadn't told the fairies to re-create this scene—just as he hadn't told them to put his face in any of the paintings—but he was glad they'd added to his instructions. He'd have to remember to bring them a couple more steak dinners. Soon.

The fairy dust painting faded slowly, leaving only the darkening sky. Finally Candice turned to him.

"How did you do that?"

Her eyes were alive and her face was slightly flushed. He wanted to push the little table that was between them out of the way and take her in his arms and kiss her until his touch was what made her eyes sparkle and her face flush.

"Magic," he said.

"But magic doesn't work on me."

"It worked on you tonight." He took her hand and kissed her palm again. "Maybe you just needed the right partner to find your magic."

"Or maybe your magic is so strong that even I can't stop it."

"I like that. I like that anything about me could be strong enough to attract you."

"Everything about you attracts me," she said, her voice low and sexy.

"Show me. Show me how much," he said.

Without speaking she stood up and led him into her house, through the cozy kitchen, the comfortably decorated den, and into her bedroom.

"I want to undress you," she said. "Is that okay with you?"

He bent and kissed her softly on the lips. "Anything you want is okay with me, as long as you still want me."

"I can't imagine not wanting you," she said, guiding him over so that he stood beside her bed while she sat on the edge of it. He was wearing a black pullover, and she skimmed it up his body and over his head, letting her fingers trail lightly down from his shoulders over his naked chest and abdomen, loving the way his body shivered at her touch. Then she unbuttoned his jeans, taking her time to slowly unzip them while her lips teased his chest and her fingers caressed the hard lump that was pushing against his pants. When she finally got his pants undone she stood, and then, hooking her fingers in his waistband, slid the jeans down, pressing her body against his as she did so.

On her knees in front of him, she took him in her hands. He was hard and hot and his body jerked and quivered under her hands. When she closed her mouth around him he moaned her name, and had to lean against the bed to stay standing.

"Your mouth," he rasped, "is a dream. A very sexy dream."

"Wet dream?" she asked when she paused.

"Oh, God, yes," he moaned.

She laughed, but before she could take him in her mouth again, he pulled her to her feet and in one quick movement, lifted her onto the bed. Lying beside her he unbuttoned her shirt.

"Now that's sexy," he said, running his finger lightly over the delicate white lace bra. "Too many women think red or black or some other godawful bright color is what men want. I don't know about other men," he murmured, "but I think white is the sexiest. You can see right through it." He circled her nipple with his finger, causing it to harden. "But there's something innocent about it. Like what it's covering has been waiting just for you." He bent over her, taking her nipple into his mouth right through the sheer lace of the bra.

Candice's breath left her in a rush. "My panties match," were the only words her lust-clouded mind could form.

Justin moved from her bra to unbutton the short cotton skirt she was wearing. He pulled it down and then knelt between her legs, gazing down at her body. She watched him closely and suddenly saw herself reflected in the desire that was so clear on his face, and knew she'd never again think of herself as old or fat or frumpy.

"Feel what you do to me," he whispered.

He took her hand and pressed it to his chest so that she could feel the racing of his heart. She let her fingers rest there for a moment, and then held the hand that had so recently covered hers against her breast.

"Feel what you do to me," she echoed.

"It's good that we're in this together," he said. "I don't think I could stand feeling all of this alone."

"You're not alone," Candice said.

"Give me a chance," Justin said. "Say you'll take me seriously, even though you think I'm too damn young."

"Justin, I don't expect—" she started.

"Expect!" he blurted. "Can't you just expect magic? Even if it's never happened to you before, can't you let me prove to you that there's more than one kind of magic in this world, and that we can make it happen together?" He leaned down and cupped her face between his hands. "I want you, Candice Cox. Not just tonight. I want you in my life. Let me make you love me."

His words scared and thrilled her. She should tell him no. Or she should lie to him and say yeah, whatever, so that they could have more good sex, and then send him on his way. But she didn't want to. It might be stupid. It probably wouldn't work. But Candice wanted more than anything else to take a chance on loving Justin. Unexpected tears came to her eyes when she answered him.

"I've waited a long time to feel like this, Justin. I can't let you go now," she said.

He smiled and wiped the dampness from her cheeks. "Well, you had to wait for me to grow up."

"Hush and kiss me." She pulled him down to her.

Soon neither of them could talk anymore. All they could do was feel.

* 8 *

Candice slept till noon again the next day—this time curled up against Justin's body. And she awoke to his gentle caresses and they made love slowly, whispering erotic secrets as morning gave way to afternoon. They'd said good-bye like lovers had for centuries, with lots of long looks and lingering touches.

And tomorrow . . . they were meeting tomorrow. He'd wanted to see her again that night, but as he'd been kissing her good-bye for about the zillionth time, his cell phone had interrupted them. He'd taken the call, albeit reluctantly, and after he'd hung up he'd apologized, saying that it was a call from his family's restaurant. They needed him to go to Denver tonight because . . . hell. She didn't remember exactly what he'd said. She'd been too busy floating on a cloud of sexual satisfaction.

But that wasn't all it was, Candice reminded herself that evening as she poured a glass of white wine and took it to her writing desk. She was floating on more than a sex cloud. She really liked him. Her lips tilted up in a secret smile as she remembered the text message she'd received from him not long ago. It had simply said:

Did my heart love till now? Forswear it, sight! For I ne'er saw true beauty till this night.

First DeMass, then Frost, and now Shakespeare! He was smart and interesting and so sexy she wanted to begin at his mouth and lick her way down his body . . . and then back up again. And he wanted her to be in his life—to love him. No matter how improbable or impossible, she found herself wanting the same thing. She sighed happily and sipped her wine. Creative juices flowing (along with all the rest of them), she picked up her pencil and reread the poem she'd started.

Keep your Errol Flynns, Paul Newmans, Mel Gibsons
all puppets—empty masquerades.
Tom, Dick, and Harry, too
the boy next door
I want no more.

You ask, what now?
Well, love comes with the night,
in the most inexplicable places
leaving the most unexplainable traces.
You see . . . a wolfman is the man for me!
True, hair in the sink is copious,

She grinned at where she'd stopped and, inspired, started writing.

and the house at night tends to be a mess.
But

The ringing phone jarred her. The caller ID said Tawdry, Godiva.

"Well, hi there, girlfriend. Long time no hear from." Godiva's voice was smug. "So, has anything new come . . . uh, *up* recently?"

Candice's breath came out in a rush. "Shit! You know! How the hell do you know?" Then she gasped, a horrible feeling lodging in her stomach. "Oh, no! Did you do it, Godiva?"

"Do what?"

"Don't play innocent witch with me. How did you manage it? Magic doesn't work on me."

"It might not work on you, but it definitely works on werewolves."

"You made him want me!" she shrieked, feeling even sicker.

"Certainly not." Godiva sounded offended. "All I did was to cast a lupine drawing spell right after the last time we talked. If it caught a wolf who didn't find you attractive, he would have never approached you. Think of it like baiting a hook. If the worm—which was you—wasn't juicy and tender and appealing to the fish—or in this case, werewolf—he would never taste the bait."

"Oh." Candice grinned, feeling so relieved she was weak-kneed.

"Details, please."

"Let's just say this worm has been well eaten."

They both dissolved into giggles.

"And," Candice said breathlessly, "I'm meeting him again tomorrow. Godiva, baby, he's quoting poetry to me! *Poetry!* And he made the stupid fairies make art for me. Can you believe it? He said he wants to worship me like a goddess, and, honey, let me tell you. I definitely can't get enough of that kind of attention! But it's more than just how completely sexy he is. He's smart and funny *and* totally into me. And, Godiva, I *really* like him."

"Sounds fabulous! Who is he?"

"You mean you don't know?"

"No. I told you—I just baited the hook. I had no idea which wolf would bite."

"Oh, Godiva, it's so deliciously naughty. He's *young*, and"—

she dropped her voice to a whisper—"he's an ex-student of mine."

"Oh, my Goddess! How wickedly yummy. Give. Who is he?" Godiva gushed.

"Justin Woods," she gushed.

"Who?"

"Justin Woods. You know, his family are the werewolves who own Red Riding Hood's."

"Oh, Goddess."

"What? What's wrong? I know he's young, but it's not like he's still a teenager—which would be totally and completely disgusting—he's twenty-six. And a half. Practically twenty-seven."

"Oh, Goddess."

"Godiva Tawdry, stop saying that and tell me what's wrong!" Candice was beginning to feel sick again.

"I should have known," Godiva groaned. "But how could I have known? I didn't think it would be *him*."

"Godiva. Tell me."

The witch drew a deep breath and then blurted out, "He's a slut."

"What?!"

"He's the most promiscuous werewolf in town—or out of town, for that matter. The pack tramp. Truly a dog in all the worst connotations of the word."

"Oh, no . . ."

"Oh, yes. I promise you. My Romeo has told me all about him. He's the pack joke. Thinks he's some kind of furry Don Juan. He's always licking coeds and cheerleaders and whatnot."

"Cheerleaders!"

"I'm so sorry, Candice."

"And all that stuff he said to me . . ."

"You mean about making a woman orgasm with his mouth?" Candice gasped in horror.

"Let me guess—he licked your foot and sucked your toes?" Godiva said.

"Yes," Candice squeaked.

"That's his move. He does that with all the girls— wolves—whatever."

"I may puke." She put her hand to her forehead and closed her eyes. How could she have been so damn gullible? "How about the poetry he quoted and the fairy art? Does he use that on all of his victims, too?"

"I don't remember hearing about that, but hey, come on! Just forget about it." Godiva forced perkiness into her voice. "You had a good time, right? A little fling—an unclogging of your pipes."

"He played me for a fool." Candice's voice was quiet and intense. She let her anger build. As long as she was thoroughly pissed she could keep the hurt from blossoming like a black flower inside of her.

"No, he's just—"

Candice cut her off. "No, Godiva! It wasn't all fun and games—he made it appear to be more than that. I should have known . . . I should have been smarter, but he's not going to get away with it. I said I was too old for this kind of shit, and I am. But not because I'm dried up and unattractive. I'm too old to be lied to and manipulated. So tell me the truth. He's obviously not going on a supply run for his family tonight. I want you to find out from Romeo what he's really doing."

"Uh, if I do and I tell you, what are you going to do?"

"Well, my witchy friend, I can sum that up in one word. Retribution."

He should never have agreed to meet the twins at the full moon party. It didn't matter that his intentions had been right. He hadn't told Candice the truth, which had been bothering him ever since the family restaurant supply run lie had blurted from his mouth. He shouldn't have answered the damn phone, but he'd been feeling so good there with Candice—so right—that when the phone rang he . . .

He what? He'd answered it because he'd wanted to yell from the mountainside that he'd FOUND SOMEONE INCRED-IBLE! In retrospect that seemed stupid and immature. And instead of telling the world about Candice, he'd quickly agreed to meet Brittney and Whitney at the party that night. There was little he wouldn't have agreed to just to get them off the phone before Candice heard their silly female voices on the line and dumped him right then and there.

And actually going to the party hadn't seemed stupid—not until he'd stepped into the forest and felt the moon's call on his blood. He'd answered that call automatically, embracing the sweet savage pleasure and heat of sinew and bone changing and re-forming with the power of the beast. He'd meant to show up long enough to tell the twins—and any of the other numerous females he'd pleasured—that he was officially taking himself off the market. He meant to make a clean split with his old life, so that he could begin his new one. Earlier that day he'd even gone online and looked up the Denver Art Institute. Then he'd actually begun a sketch. Just a woman's eyes. They were green and framed with thick blonde lashes and soft laugh lines. . . .

Thinking of Candice, Justin let the moon caress his fur as he raised his muzzle to the sky. Surrounded by young wolves who were breaking off into intimate groups, he howled his passion for Candice into the night.

The full moon was so white against the absolute black of the starless sky that it almost looked silver. Sitting at the edge of the clearing, Candice breathed deeply of the warm night air and waited. It wasn't long before she heard them approaching through the trees. They weren't being stealthy—there was no reason for it. They were being young and uninhibited and very, very horny.

Godiva had been right (again). It was easy to tell which of the wolves was Justin. That thick sand-colored pelt was as distinctive as his eyes (and his tongue).

She stood up and stepped into the clearing. Keeping the hand that clutched the collar hidden behind her back, she cocked her hip and shook out her hair. With a sexy purr in her voice, she called to him.

"Justin, come here, boy!" The big wolf sitting between two blonde bitches who were drooling over him (literally) while he howled at the sky cocked his ears at her. Candice ran her hand suggestively over her body. "I have something special for you that I just couldn't wait till tomorrow to give you."

With an enthusiastic woof, he bounded toward her, his all-too-familiar tongue lolling. With one quick movement, she dropped to her knees beside him and slipped the heavy-duty choke collar around his throat.

"Arruff?" he said, staring up at her in confusion.

"Tonight you're coming with me," she whispered. When the bitches yapped at her, she grinned over her shoulder at them. "Don't worry. I'll give him back to you—but not till I've had my way with him."

He whined and squirmed as she dragged him to the Jeep

she'd borrowed from Godiva. No damn way his hairy ass was going to fit in her lovely little Mini—even if she did allow dogs to ride with her, which she definitely didn't.

"Don't bother with the whining and big doggie eyes. They're not going to work," she told him. "And remember, my magic is nonmagic. You can't change as long as I'm close to you. But isn't that convenient? I hear that your favorite position is very close to a woman. Any woman. So get comfortable, fur-face."

"Thank goodness I caught you before you closed, Doctor." Candice smiled as she dragged the whining wolf into the veterinary clinic.

"Is there something wrong with your . . ." The vet hesitated, narrowing his eyes at the wolf.

"Dog," Candice supplied innocently. "Yes, there is something wrong with my dog. I need you to perform emergency surgery."

"Really? He looks healthy to me." The vet reached down and ruffled the "dog's" sandy fur.

Justin whined pitifully.

"You're a big boy, aren't you?" the vet said.

"He certainly thinks he is—which explains the emergency. I need you to cut off his . . ." Candice paused, glanced at Justin, then dropped her voice and whispered into the vet's ear.

"Well, I don't know. It's pretty late. I was just closing," he said.

"Surely you can fit him in. Pretty please, Doc?" She fluttered her lashes at him.

The vet smiled and shrugged. "I suppose I could for my favorite teacher. Go, Fairies!"

"Go, Fairies!" Candice chimed in automatically.

"If you wait here, I'll take him in the back and be done in no time."

"No! I mean, I'll come with you. If I don't stay close to him he'll change . . . into something that might surprise you."

"But you won't want to watch!"

"Of course not," she assured him. "I'll stay in the room, but I have a poem I need to finish, so I'll be concentrating on that while you take care of his little *problems*."

"Suit yourself, teacher," the vet said. "Bring him back."

Justin began to growl.

"Doc, I think we need a muzzle."

Candice settled on a metal folding chair not too far from the operating room table, careful to keep her back to the busy veterinarian and his unwillingly drugged patient. She ignored the tight, sick feeling in her stomach and, while Justin was being prepped, she picked up her pencil and smiled grimly as she finished her poem.

CANDY COX AND THE BIG BAD (WERE)WOLF

Keep your Errol Flynns, Paul Newmans, Mel Gibsons
all puppets—empty masquerades.
Tom, Dick, and Harry, too
the boy next door
I want no more.
You ask, what now?
Well, love comes with the night,
in the most inexplicable places
leaving the most unexplainable traces.
You see . . . a wolfman is the man for me!
True, hair in the sink is copious,
and the house at night tends to be a mess.
But if that wolfman breaks my heart,
if he thinks that we should part,
I'll wait until the moon is waxing full
that magic time when his change is soon,
(my love is quite helpless then, as a puppy . . .
baby . . . body in a mortuary)
I'd collar that fur-faced gigolo
and make a timely visit to the Vet.

Ah, well, I'm sure there'll never be a need.
I haven't seen a neutered werewolf . . .

P. C. CAST

Candice glanced up at where the vet obscured her view of the sleeping, spread-eagled Justin.

. . . Yet.

As the vet picked up an evil-looking scalpel, Candice closed her notebook.

"Doc?"

The vet paused, blade hovering above the spread-eagled "dog," and glanced over his shoulder at her.

"I'm sorry. I know this is going to seem odd, but I've changed my mind."

He frowned at her.

She gave a purposefully silly, girly-girl laugh. "Oopsie, sorry. I guess I just can't go through with it, no matter how . . . uh, naughty he's been. I'll still pay you for the neutering, though. Don't worry." She fished her checkbook out of her purse and hastily wrote the vet a check. Then she nodded at the sleeping Justin. "How long will he be out?"

"A couple hours."

"Perfect. Can you help me lift him into my car?"

* 9 *

Justin woke up in the ditch not far from the clearing where the party was still in full swing, as evidenced by the randy growls and breathless giggles that drifted on the night air. At first he was totally disoriented. His mouth felt like a bird had shit in it and he had a killer headache. What the hell? He'd gone to the party as a farewell to his old life, and then . . .

With a terrified yelp, his memory rushed back. Commanding his human form to come to him, he sat up, gasping and reaching between his legs. All there! He was all there.

What had happened? Why had Candice freaked out?

But even before Justin found the neatly folded note she'd left staked to the ground beside him with . . . he shuddered . . . something that looked disturbingly like a scalpel, he knew what had happened. Someone had told her about him. He was fully aware of his bad reputation. He'd never really given a shit. Until now. He opened the piece of notebook paper. The full moon had brightened the sky enough for him to easily read her bold writing.

Girls might think it's cute or exciting to be with a man who collects lovers like a dog collects fleas. Well, that's just one of the many differences between girls and women. Gigolo men piss grown women off. I'm a grown woman. The game you played with me pisses me off. I suggest you stick to girls. Next time you may lose more than a few orgy hours. Keep in mind, "Heaven has no rage like love to hatred turned, nor hell a fury like a woman scorned." Ah, to hell with that poetic crap. Basically, I wanted to say, GO FUCK YOURSELF, JUSTIN!

When he returned to wolf form he didn't notice the sensual stir of his morphing flesh, and he didn't rush back to the clearing to pair up with an eager young wolf to reassure himself that everything was still in working order. Instead he padded slowly home—the garage apartment his parents pretended to rent to him as part of his salary and benefits at the restaurant, which felt as empty and meaningless as his life had become.

"You should be almost done with that awful poetry class, right?" Godiva asked her friend.

Candice was sitting on her balcony, arm resting against her little table, pad and pencil beside her. She stared out at the forest while she propped the phone against her shoulder and kept doodling on her notebook paper. "Yep. Almost."

"And that means the whole MFA is almost done, right?"

"Yep. Almost."

"And snow is almost done falling out of that giant flying rabbit's ass, right?"

"Yep. Al—" Candice frowned, realizing what Godiva had really said. "Don't be such a smart-ass."

"You know, I hear he's back in town."

"I don't want to talk about it."

"So don't talk—just listen. He's back in town, but werewolf gossip has it that he's only here temporarily. Seems he's just come to collect some of his stuff to take back to his new apartment in Denver."

"And why should I care?"

Godiva kept talking as if Candice hadn't spoken. "Word also has it that he's still not slutting around. No parties. No orgies. No cheerleaders. Not even the slightest hint of a girl-friend, wolf or not."

"Godiva! I do not give a shit. I haven't talked to him in weeks."

"Well, maybe you should!"

"I cannot believe you're saying that. You're the one who told me what a slut he was. And I saw it with my own eyes. He lied to me and was fucking every bitch in sight that night."

"Girlfriend, I told you what Romeo told me—that several werewolves told him that Justin wasn't doing anyone that night. And, as far as my excellent gossip network—which includes forest fairies, and you know those little shits live for gossip and red meat—can tell, Justin Woods has not been with anyone since the three dates he had with you."

"Two dates. And one of them wasn't even official."

"Whatever. I think you should call him."

"What! I am *not* going to call that boy."

"Oh, give it up. You know very well he's no boy."

"Again I say whatever. And he knows my phone number. If he wanted to talk to me, he'd call me."

"Candice Cox, may I please remind you that the last time you interacted with him you almost had his balls cut off, you dumped him in a ditch, and you left a scary revenge note, complete with a literary quote and a go-fuck-yourself."

"He lied to me."

"True, and circumstantial evidence pointed to his definitely being an asswipe. But since then he has behaved respectably, by either man or wolf standards."

Candice sighed. "I can't call him. I feel like an idiot."

"Do you want me to cast a little—"

"Hell, no! Godiva Tawdry, promise me right now that you will not put any kind of love spell, or anything like a love spell, on Justin."

"Okay! I promise. But I still think you should call him." She brightened. "Hey, I could have Romeo talk to—"

"No! God, I feel like I'm trapped in a dream where I'm back in high school trying to figure out my locker combination and realizing I'm butt-ass naked. Just leave it alone, Godiva. If Justin wanted to see me again, he'd figure out a way to do it." And she knew it was true. Candice had only been with him for a short time, but she believed in his tenacity. He'd set his sights on seducing her, and he'd certainly accomplished his goal. If he had any desire to talk to her or see her, he'd get it done. But even though his behavior had changed drastically since the night she'd almost had him neutered, he had stayed completely away from her. Not that she cared.

"Candice?"

"Oh, sorry, what did you say?"

"I asked what your last poetry assignment was about."

"We have to write two poems about heartbreak. One free verse. One sonnet. And neither can be clichéd."

"Oh, a real uplifting assignment."

"Yeah, it's just one laugh after another over here."

"Are they done?"

"Almost. I just have to finish tweaking the couplet to conclude the sonnet. Then I'm going to set them aside for a day or so, and do a quick rewrite before I have to turn them in next week."

"After you do that, why don't you and I get all dressed up and go into Denver for some excellent Italian food? I'll even drive."

"I'm not flying on that damn broom of yours."

"I said *drive*."

"I'll think about it," Candice said.

Godiva paused. She was almost afraid to ask the next question, but she knew she had to. Her talent was, after all, healing. Resolutely, she said, "Candy, what happened with Justin really did break your heart, didn't it?" It took her friend several seconds to answer her.

"Yeah," she finally whispered into the phone. "Isn't that stupid?"

"No, it's not stupid. It's what can happen when we love someone, and you have rarely let yourself love anyone."

"Ironic, isn't it? And I'm the one who's been married a zillion times."

"You didn't really love any of the ex-husnumbers. But there was something about Justin that got to you."

"I wish . . . ," Candy began.

"What, honey?"

"I wish your magic worked on me."

"So do I, honey. So do I."

After she hung up, Godiva sat staring at the phone a long time. There had to be some way she could help her friend. After all, it was her fault this whole thing had happened. First, she'd cast the drawing spell that had brought them together. Then she'd spilled the beans about Justin's promiscuous ways. Who knew the wolf was going to have some big, hairy epiphany and learn to zip his pants? And now the gossip tree said that he was really getting his shit together. Seems he was spearheading the acquisition of a new restaurant for his family, and the eavesdropping fairies, who seemed to have a real soft spot for the wolf, had even heard whispers that he'd reenrolled in college. Was it just her? Wasn't it obvious to everyone that Justin was trying to make himself worthy of Candice?

And Candice was moping around like she'd been stuck in a classroom with the horrid Desdaine triplets (Godiva shuddered—Goddess! What a wretched thought! Those girls were the brat pack.). Something had to be done.

Maybe if Justin knew how miserable Candice was . . . maybe then he'd call her and they'd live happily ever after!

But she'd promised Candice she wouldn't cast any love spells on him. Godiva tapped her long fingernail against her chin. Then she smiled. Candice was writing poems about heartbreak.

What if Justin were to read them? He wouldn't know that they were an assignment! He'd just think she was pining over him—which she was. That was it; the fairies would be only too happy to help. . . .

Humming to herself, Godiva began gathering four-leaf clovers . . . the little dried white things from the tops of dandelions . . . a pinch of frog snot . . . and various other delightful things she would need for the spell. . . .

Candice rubbed her neck and stretched. Well, the couplet that ended the sonnet was done. Good thing, too, it was getting dark and she should move inside from her porch. But she didn't get up. She liked sitting out there. And it wasn't because she remembered another evening on the porch, one that had been filled with hope and magic and love. . . .

No. It was just that the woods were quiet, and their somberness reflected her recent mood. It was nice to sit out on her balcony and write, even if what she wrote was damn depressing. She lifted the paper that had the final draft of both poems written on it and shook her head sadly. They were good. She knew it. But if they did evoke feelings, the feelings would be sadness, loss, longing. . . .

She put the paper down, remembering how not long ago she had dreamed of writing things that evoked brighter emotions.

What was wrong with her? So she'd had a little fling that

had ended abruptly and, quite frankly, not very well. It was ridiculous that it was still making her feel this sad. She closed her eyes and rested her head against the back of the chair. What was it about Justin that stayed with her? Was it just because he'd been so damn handsome? That couldn't be it. Ex-husband numbers one and four had been very handsome men. Well, was it the sex? No. Ex-husband numbers one and three had been fantastic in the sack. She'd gotten over all of them, more easily than she usually cared to admit. So why was Justin still haunting her dreams?

Against her closed eyes the warm evening breeze had picked up. It felt good, almost like a caress against her skin. It made her think of the summer, when dandelions dried and their little white heads blew all over fields of four-leaf clovers. She sighed and relaxed, feeling suddenly sleepy. . . .

. . . Until she heard the wild flapping and opened her eyes in time to see her homework papers being lifted by the crazy wind. She leaped up, grabbing at papers, sure she saw translucent pastel wings fluttering in among the notebook pages as her poetry scattered out into the forest.

"Fucking fairies!" she screamed, running after the trail of paper.

An hour later she had still not found the final drafts of both poems. Grumbling about hanging sticky flypaper and a giant bug zapper to get rid of the fairy problem, she gave up, resigning herself to rewriting the finals again. At least she'd just finished both poems that day. It shouldn't be too hard for her to remember exactly what she'd written. . . .

He'd gone for a walk. Justin hadn't even understood why, but all of a sudden it had been very important that he take a walk in the woods, and before he knew it, he was heading south. Toward her house. He'd just realized how close he was to her little log cabin when the wind changed directions and, in a flutter of iridescent wings, two papers blew straight into his hands. He felt a jolt at the familiar writing.

Poetry . . . her poetry!

Then he started reading, and his heart clenched. Candice's words were like a mirror of what was going on inside him. Could it be? Could she really care as much as he did? He read on, and images began to form in his mind, and with them a plan. Maybe, just maybe, he could find a way to reach her.

* 10 *

To some people it might seem counterproductive to jog to town simply to eat a triple fudge banana split. To Candice it made perfect sense. She sat outside the One-Stop Mart and tried to tune out the sounds of the arguing Desdaine triplets as they fought over God knew what. Those monsters were always into something. And that poor sweet preacher, what was her name? Pastor Harmony? She'd somehow gotten trapped in there with those little demons. Candice could hear the woman trying to end the argument before any of the three little terrors could permanently disable some hapless passerby, which was just damn brave of the preacher. No wonder everyone said she was honestly nice—that she accepted everyone no matter how magical or nonmagical (or how disdainfully horrid).

Something crashed inside the store and Candice cringed. How old were those brats now? Eleven? Twelve? She'd damn sure better be out of teaching before, like a plague of locusts, they descended upon Mysteria High. Just another reason to land that fabulous job as an editor in Denver. Candice ate her ice cream slowly, dreaming of the romantic possibilities of her future profession. She'd have three-martini lunches with authors. She'd wear amazing clothes and have a loft near downtown. She'd discover the next Nora Roberts!

"Candice! There you are. Holy bat shit! You will not believe what the vampire is displaying in his gallery!" Godiva rushed up to her friend, her large round bosoms heaving with excitement.

"More porno dressed up as art?" Candice said, interest definitely aroused. She was always up for some full-frontal male nudity. Actually, it might be just the thing to help her get over the Justin Blues. Unfortunately, Godiva shook her head.

"No. It's not porn."

"Damn. Then what's the big deal? You know I don't like those bloody pictures the vamps think are cool. I don't know why vampires are so into art, anyway. You'd think they'd choose a more, I don't know, nocturnal profession."

"Candice! Just come with me. I cannot begin to explain what you're going to see."

"Can I finish my banana split first?"

"Bring it. This can't wait."

Grumbling, Candice let Godiva shoo her down Main Street to Mysteria's only art gallery, Dark Shadows. A crowd was gathered around the front display window, and as she got closer, she realized that all of them were staring in the window, and they all were crying.

Crying? The exhibition was so bad it was making the populace cry? Sheesh.

Godiva grabbed her arm and shoved her forward so she could get a better look. At first she was so completely distracted by the beauty of the pieces and the amazing talent of the artist that she didn't understand exactly what it was she was seeing. There were two watercolor paintings on display. Her immediate impression of them was that they were dream images, and they vaguely brought to mind Michael Parks's sexy fantasy work. One was of a woman who was in a cage that looked like it had been carved from ice. All around the outside of the walls of ice were big tufts of a delicately leafed plant in full purple bloom. *Lavender*, she thought. *They're bunches of blooming lavender.* Candice looked more closely at the woman in the center of the cage. She was sitting on the floor, with one hand pressed against the nearest translucent wall, almost as if she were trying to push her way out. She was wearing only a white hooded cloak. Parts of her shapely bare legs were showing, but her face was in shadows—all except her eyes, which were large and mesmerizing with their mossy green sadness. There was something else about her eyes. . . .

Candice shifted her attention to the other painting. It, too, was amazingly rich in detail and color. It showed a woman sleeping on a bed that was in the middle of what looked to be a dark room in a castle. Mist, or maybe fog, hung around the bed, further obscuring the woman. A single tall, narrow window slit let in two pearl-winged doves, as well as a ray of moonlight, which fell across the bed, illuminating the side of the woman's face so that a single tear at the corner of her eye was visible. This woman's face was also in shadow. Her blonde hair spilled around her on the dark bed, drawing Candice's eye. What was it about her hair?

Then she realized that displayed beside each painting was a framed poem. She pushed her way farther through the sobbing crowd until she was so close to the window that she pressed her fingers against the cold glass. Candice began reading the elaborate calligraphy of the first poem.

> Come, icy wall of silence
> encase my weary heart
> protect me with your hold, hard strength
> till no pain may trespass here.
> Make still my battered feelings
> within your protective fortress
> safe
> request I this sanctuary from life's storm.

But, what of this ensorcelled heart?
Will it struggle so encased?
Or will walls forged to keep harm out
cause love's flame to flicker low
till silence meant as soothing balm
does its work too well, and
no more breath can escape
to melt the fortress of frozen tears.

Candice couldn't breathe. She felt as if someone had punched her in the stomach. Frantically, her eyes went to the second poem. It was a sonnet, and it was written in the same meticulous calligraphy.

The dreamer dreamed a thousand wasted years
Captive of wondrous images she slept
Swathed close in sighs and moans and blissful tears
Reliving promises made, but not kept.

The moon's deft watch through narrow casement fell
Its silvered light caressed her silken face
Like a dove's soft wings colored gray and shell
Shadowy thoughts frozen in time and place.

He watched her breath like silver mist depart
And he longed to join her murderous sleep

But truth rare listens to the wounded heart
Hence even hero souls must sometimes weep.

Now love's pinions can never more take flight,
Entombed forever in grief's endless night.

"They're mine," Candice whispered. Her stricken voice didn't carry above the sobs of the people around her. She tore her eyes from the window and looked frantically back at Godiva, who was standing at the edge of the crowd crying softly. She raised her voice so that her friend could hear her. "They're my poems, Godiva. I wrote them."

"Who said that?!"

Heads swiveled to the tall gaunt figure standing in the doorway of the gallery. Barnabas Vlad (a name everyone in Mysteria knew he had absolutely, beyond any doubt, *not* been born with) was swathed head to toe in black, holding a small lacy black parasol, and wearing huge blue blocker reflective sunglasses.

"Who said that she is the poetess?"

"That would be me," Candice said reluctantly.

All the heads then swiveled in her direction and Candice heard weepy murmurs of *Oh, they're so wonderful,* and *They break my heart, but I love them,* and *I have to have one of my own and the art that goes with it!*

Barnabas pointed one finger (fully covered in a black opera-length glove) at Candice. "You must come with me at once!" The vampire turned and scuttled through the gallery door.

Candice couldn't move. Everyone was staring at her.

"Let's go!" Godiva pushed her toward the gallery door, ignoring the gawking crowd. Then, still sobbing softly, she added, "And no way are you going in there without me."

Candice had been in the gallery before. It was decidedly on the dark side—walls and floor black instead of the usual clean white of most galleries. It was never well lit, and it was always too damn cold. But she liked the art exhibits, especially the gay pride exhibits Barnabas liked to have. She could appreciate full-frontal male nudity, even if it couldn't appreciate her.

"Back here, ladies." Barnabas called breathily from the rear office. Godiva and Candice exchanged glances. Both shrugged and followed the vampire's voice.

"You're sure it's your poetry?" Godiva whispered, wiping her eyes and blowing her nose.

"Of course I'm sure," she hissed at her friend. "How could you even ask me that! They're the poems about heartbreak I wrote a week or so ago for that poetry class."

"Well, it's just that . . ." But they'd come to Barnabas's office so Godiva clamped her mouth shut.

"Ladies, I'm charmed. Come in and sit, *s'il vous plaît*." Barnabas fluttered his long fingers at the two delicate pink silk Louis XIV chairs that sat regally before his ornately carved mahogany desk. When they were seated the vampire launched into a breathy speech in his trademark poorly rendered French accent. "Do *pardon* my abruptness out there, but it's been wretchedly stressful since I put up that new display. That is no excuse for *moi* rudeness, though. It is just such a shock—such a surprise. *Mon dieu!* Who would have imagined that such a magnificent discovery would have been made at my humble gallery? Oh! How rude of me. Introductions are in order. I am Barnabas Vlad, the proprietor of this humble *galerie d'art*." He peered at Godiva for a moment, squinting his eyes so that his iridescent pink eye shadow creased unattractively. Then his expression cleared. "Ah, *oui oui oui*! I do know you. Are you not Godiva Tawdry, one of the Tawdry witches?"

Godiva looked pleased at her notoriety. "*Oui!*" she said. Now that she'd stopped crying she was able to appreciate the humor of the undead guy's foppishly fake Frenchness.

He turned to Candice with a smile that showed way too many long, sharp teeth. "And you are our poetess! You look familiar to me, *madam*, but I'm sorry to say that I have misplaced your name."

"I'm Candice Cox," she said.

The vampire's pleasant expression instantly changed to confusion. "*Mais non!* It is not possible!"

"Okay, this is really starting to piss me off. I wrote the poems a week or so ago for an online class I'm taking for my master's. I can prove it. I turned them in last Friday. Now I want to know how you got them, who this artist is who has illustrated them, and why you all"—here she paused to glare at Godiva—"think it's so impossible that I wrote them. I may be a high school teacher, but I do have a brain!"

"*Madam!* I meant no disrespect." The vampire definitely looked flustered. "It is just . . ." He dabbed at his upper lip with a lacy black hankie before going on. "Are you not the English teacher whose magic is nonmagic?"

"Yes," Candice ground from between gritted teeth.

"Then that is why it is impossible that you have written the poems."

"What the hell—" Candice sputtered and started to get up, but Godiva's firm hand on her arm stopped her.

"Candice," Godiva said. "The poems have magic."

"*Exactement!*" Barnabas said, clearly relieved that Godiva had stepped in.

"Magic? But how? I don't understand," Candice said.

"You saw the people. Your poems made them cry. They made *me* cry. When I looked at the paintings and then read your words, I thought my heart would break with sadness. It was awful—and wonderful." Godiva teared up again just thinking about it.

"That is how everyone has been reacting," Barnabas said. "Since I put them on display this morning. Weeping and blubbering, blubbering and weeping."

"But where did you get them?" Candice felt as if she'd

just gotten off a Tilt-a-Whirl and couldn't quite get her bearings.

"They were in a plain brown package I found by the rear door to the gallery this morning. I opened it, and my heart began to break. *Naturellement* I instantly put them on display."

"So who left the package?"

He shrugged. "It did not say. There was only this note in the package."

Candice snatched the paper from his expensively gloved fingers. Typed on a plain white piece of regular computer paper it said:

> *If the poet would like to work with me again I would be willing.*
> *Tell her that I will meet her here at the gallery tonight at sunset.*

"But there's no signature or anything," Candice said.

"Artists." Barnabas sighed and rolled his eyes.

"Okay, none of this makes any sense. The artist seems to know who I am, but I have no idea who this person is, how he or she got my poems. I mean, I just wrote them for the online class. I typed them into the computer, attached them to my e-mail, and sent them to the creative writing professor. Then I put the originals into a file labeled with the proper class. I suppose someone at the university could have gotten to them. The only other copies were blown away one day in a freak windstorm."

Godiva shifted guiltily in her chair.

Candice shot her a narrowed look. "What do you know about this, Godiva Tawdry?"

"Nothing!" she said quickly.

"So you did not print them in such lovely calligraphy?" Barnabas asked.

"No! Not even my handwritten copies looked anything like those." Candice got up and marched to the front window. She yanked both framed poems from the easels on which they were displayed. As an afterthought she made little shooing motions at the gawking, crying people. Then she hurried back to Barnabas's office.

"Let me see them," Godiva said. Candice gave them to her and the witch studied the poems. "This is hand-lettered with a calligraphy quill—nothing computer-generated about it." She kept staring at the poetry, and suddenly her eyes widened. "It's not working!"

"What?" Candice asked.

"The magic. I'm not feeling anything." She looked apologetically at her friend as she handed the poems back. "They're perfectly lovely poems, but I'm not crying."

"So the magic's gone?" She should have known it. No way would she really have magic. She glanced at Barnabas. The vampire looked stricken.

"Wait. I have an idea," Godiva said. Flouncing herself over to the window, she grabbed one of the paintings, noting that all the criers had dried up and drifted away. She returned with the picture. "I need the poem that goes with this one."

Candice looked at the green-eyed woman in the cave of ice, and was in the process of handing the free verse poem to her friend when she gasped and stared at the painting.

"The eyes! I knew there was something about them. She has my eyes."

Barnabas looked from the painting to the teacher. "*Mon dieu!* You are right, *madam*."

"The other one has your hair," Godiva said.

"Holy shit," Candice said.

"Give me the poem."

Candice let Godiva take it out of her numb fingers. The witch held the poem up beside the picture. Almost immediately the vampire started to sniffle. Through his tears he said rapturously, "It has returned! The magic has returned!"

"It never went away," Godiva said. "It just doesn't work without the paintings."

"That is weird as hell," Candice said.

"*Madam*," Barnabas gushed breathily into the silence, "I would like to commission you and the artist for twelve more poetry paintings. And I would be willing to pay you this amount of money." He scribbled a number down on a piece of pink notepaper and slid it over the desk to Candice.

She picked up the paper. She blinked. And blinked again.

She could not believe the amount of zeros on the paper. "You want to pay me this for twelve poems?"

"*Mais non!*" He looked offended. "I would pay you this for each of the twelve poems, as long as your artist agrees to illustrate them. *Naturellement*, I would pay the artist the same commission. I have already called my brother in Denver. As soon as you and the artist *fini*, we will have a grand opening exhibit in the city that will be *très extraordinaire!*"

Candice wasn't sure she could breathe. "But I don't even know who the artist is."

"We're idiots!" Godiva said. "Isn't there a signature on the paintings?"

"No, *madam sorcière*. I studied each painting for the artist's signature. What I found was odd, not a normal signature at all."

"Well, what did you find?" Candice asked, staring at the painting.

"In the bottom right corner of each is a miniature reproduction of a full moon. That is the only signature the artist left."

Candice sighed. "Looks like I'll be here at sunset to meet this mysterious artist."

"But I think you should go home and change first," Godiva said. "Those jogging shorts are frayed and you spilled banana split all over your shirt."

Candice was too busy wondering at the amazing events to notice Godiva's self-satisfied little smile.

CANDY COX AND THE BIG BAD (WERE)WOLF

· 115 ·

* 11 *

Candice was more excited than nervous. She dressed carefully, purposefully picking artsy clothes instead of the boring teacher crap that hung in the front of her closet. *A poetess!* she told herself, *I'm going to dress like a poetess.*

She chose a silk skirt that she'd bought in a funky shop in Manitou Springs the last time she'd visited the Colorado Springs area. Its scalloped hem flirted a couple of inches above her knees and it made her feel pretty and feminine. She matched a sleeveless black top with it and then hung her new necklace around her neck. It was a waterfall of amber beads and she realized that she'd bought it only because it reminded her of Justin's eyes—but she couldn't seem to help herself. *This job will help me get over him. And if it keeps up it'll be my ticket out of here. Denver, here I come!* She pointedly ignored the fact that rumor said Justin was living in Denver. It didn't matter. Denver was a big city, and she'd never run into him. She didn't hang in the coed crowd. Instead of thinking about Justin, Candice slid on a pair of strappy black sandals, gave her hair one more fluff, and rushed out to her Mini.

The sun was just setting when she pulled up in front of the gallery. She was relieved that Barnabas had taken the paintings and poetry out of the display window. She really didn't want to wade through another crowd of crying people to get to the door.

Stepping into the gallery she was met by Barnabas, who was wringing his hands.

"The artist insists on meeting alone with you, *madam*," he said. "I will go, but I will be back in *exactement* one hour to hear your decision. *Au revoir* until later, then."

"But where's the artist?"

"In the rear gallery. That is where I have hung your work." With one more worried glance around his gallery, the vampire minced out the door.

Candice straightened her shoulders and walked to the rear gallery. He was standing with his back to her, studying the two paintings that hung beside the framed poems. *He's really tall*, was her first thought. He was wearing a dark, conservative suit that fit his broad shoulders well and tapered nicely down to his waist. His thick sand-colored hair was short and neatly cut. He didn't seem to notice that she was there.

"Hi. My name is Candice Cox and I'm the poet," she said, wishing she'd given more thought to how she would introduce herself.

"I know who you are," he said without turning around.

Candice blinked. Was she so excited that her ears were playing tricks on her? That voice. She knew that voice. Didn't she?

"Why did you write these poems?" he asked.

"As an assignment for a class I'm taking." She felt the air slowly being squeezed out of her.

"Was that the only reason?" He still didn't turn around.

"No," she said softly. "When I wrote them I tried to explain how I was feeling."

"And how was that?"

"My heart had been broken. I made a stupid mistake and jumped to a conclusion that wasn't the right one."

Finally, the artist turned slowly around. His amber eyes met hers. "You weren't all that mistaken."

She couldn't believe it was really him. With his hair cut and his suit he looked . . . he looked like a man who could take on the world and win.

"I've missed you, Candy."

"Justin, I—I . . ." She tried to put together a coherent sentence while her emotions swirled.

"I'm sorry!" they said together.

"I should have given you a chance to explain," she blurted out.

"No! I shouldn't have gone to that stupid party to begin with," he said. "I want you to know that I wasn't going there to be with another woman."

"I know that," she said.

He took a couple of steps toward her. "Did I really break your heart?"

"Yes," she whispered.

"Is there any way you could let me fix it?" he asked.

"Yes," she whispered again. Then she closed the space between them and stepped into his arms. He bent to kiss her, but her words stopped him. "You're the artist!"

He smiled. "I am."

"So you found your inspiration in my poetry?"

"No. I found my inspiration in the woman whose heart finally became soft enough to be broken, and when I did I understood that separately we are just a gigolo wolf and a burned-out teacher, but together . . ." His lips gently brushed against hers.

"Together we make magic," she finished for him.

EPILOGUE

six months later

The art gallery, Dark Shadows II, was located in trendy downtown Denver, nestled between a Starbucks and a posh designer jewelry shop. It was a popular place, known for its unique exhibits and for discovering talented new artists. But even for a popular gallery, tonight's opening was busy. No, not busy—mobbed. The gallery owner, Quentin Vlad (whom everyone in Denver believed to be eccentric and odd, which was partially true . . . the other part was that he was a vampire—something that no one needed to know) was all atwitter. Dollar signs were blazing in his eyes, and he didn't even mind that he'd had to hire extra security to control the crowd. Sold! Every available piece in the exhibit had been sold within the first hour of the opening.

He could hardly believe his brother's amazing find! Who would have imagined it? A nonmagical poet and an untrained artist werewolf—put them together and they create art that evokes feelings in the people who view it *even outside the boundaries of Mysteria*!

Now that was magic.

"Fifty thousand! I'll up my offer to fifty thousand dollars!"

Quentin looked into the flushed face of the sweaty man who was staring, mesmerized, at the spectacular painting and poem that hung side by side in the central room of the gallery. "Sir, I'm sorry. I told you the first twelve times you inquired as to its price. That particular piece is part of the artist and poet's personal collection. It is not for sale."

"Everything's for sale," the man quipped. "Everything has a price."

"Not that piece."

The deep voice came from behind them. Quentin and the desperate man looked back to see a tall, handsome young man dressed in dark jeans, a T-shirt, and a black leather jacket. He had his arm around a woman who wore funky, artsy clothes.

Her thick blonde hair was loose, framing the arresting green in her eyes perfectly. She leaned into his side intimately.

"No." She smiled. "Not that piece."

He bent to kiss her and, arm in arm, they strolled into one of the other crowded rooms of the gallery.

The sweaty-faced man's gaze stayed with them a moment, but soon his eyes were drawn back to the painting and the poem—as was everyone's attention. The painting was wondrous, a blending eroticism and beauty so breathtaking that it, alone, would have been an attention-getter in any gallery. But mix it with the poem that was displayed in intricate calligraphy and framed beside it, and wondrous evolved into spectacular . . . magical. As couples read the poem they gravitated together. Lone readers sighed wistfully. Some rushed out of the gallery, already on their cell phones to their lovers. Some just stood and stared, weeping silently at what was missing in their own lives. Some, like the sweaty-faced man, decided that if they just owned the piece then somehow, miraculously, love would find its way into their lives.

"It's what I want; what I have to have," the sweaty man said to no one in particular. "It has to be my story." He looked at Quentin one last time. "I really can't buy this?"

"No, you really can't."

The man's eyes moved back to the artwork. "But maybe I can get her to forgive me—ask her for a second chance." His eyes brightened and some of the desperate flush went out of his face. Quentin decided that he must be much more attractive when he wasn't so, well, sweaty and florid. "That's it! I'm going to ask her for a second chance!" He gripped Quentin's thin hand. "Thank you, Mr. Vlad! And thank the artist and the poet, too!" Then he rushed from the gallery.

Quentin grimaced and discreetly wiped his palm on his hand-tailored Italian suit. But like everyone in the room, his eyes were pulled unerringly back to the wall where the art was exhibited. The painting was almost life-sized. The medium was textured oil, so the nudes looked rich, their skin almost alive. Their bodies were twined together in an intimate embrace—erotic yet loving—sexual and sensual. Their faces were indistinct, and Quentin thought then, as he had the first time he'd seen the piece, about the brilliance of the artist. He'd created a painting that allowed each viewer to imagine his or her own face within the scene. But the woman's hair was distinctive—thick and long and blonde. The man in the painting fisted it in his desire as it cascaded around her shoulders. Quentin shivered. Even he was not immune to the passion in the piece. His eyes shifted to the poem and, again, he was captured in the poet's web as he read:

Second Chance

Remember when it went wrong,
When the fabric of our universe tore . . . frayed . . . dissolved?

But then you turned back time
and we escaped from the prison of withered desire
I flung my arms wide and embraced
passion newborn.

Because you turned back time
I dance naked, joyously teasing the fiery sun,
safe in the knowledge that even Apollo's
warmth cannot compare to
the heat of your caresses.

When you turned back time
I found the way to nurture
soft, sweet words
in my emerald meadow
I wound around you, a clear, cooling stream
soothing and nourishing,
helping you, in turn, to feel renewed.

And in that renewing
found my own magic
with you.

Beside the poem hung a placard that told about the artist and the poet. It read:

The medium of our work is not important. It varies from piece to piece. We do not focus on techniques or styles. We simply focus on the same thing we'd like you to focus on—the true magic of love, which will always transcend time and disbelief. May all of you live happily ever after. . . .

—JUSTIN AND CANDICE WOODS

* ✳ *

IT'S IN HIS KISS . . .

(Title hummed to the tune of Cher
singing "The Shoop Shoop Song")

To Gyna Snowater
with love from P. C. Castwater.
We rock when we team up, baby!

* 1 *

"All right, we're going to start a new unit, so get out your folders and get ready to take notes," Summer said in what she liked to hope was her best Teacher Voice.

"What's the new unit, Miss S.?" called a male voice from the rear of the class.

Summer frowned. Was it disrespectful to call her Miss S.? Oh, Goddess! Another question she'd have to ask her sister on the phone tonight. She cleared her throat and tried to look severe and ten years older. "Shakespeare's *Romeo and Juliet*."

The girls in the class sighed and looked dreamy. The boys groaned.

"Hey, I hear there's sex in that play," came the same voice from the rear of the class.

"Well, yes. Actually it's a play about star-crossed lovers whose families won't let them be together," said Summer.

The girls smiled. The boys rolled their eyes.

"So that means there's sex in it. Lots, actually," Summer said before her mind caught up with her mouth.

"Cool!"

"Of course, it's all written in Elizabethan English," she hastily amended, reconnecting with the excellent control she usually had over everything she said or did.

"Sucks fairy butt," said a surly voice from the other side of the room.

"So we won't get it?" asked a cute blonde in the front row who wore a short, pink cheerleading uniform with FIGHTING FAIRIES emblazoned across her perky bosom.

"Don't worry. I'll make sure you get it," Summer said.

"Awesome!" chorused several annoying male voices, accompanied by giggles from the girls.

"Hey, Miss Smith, can we watch the movie?" asked the cheerleader.

"The one that shows Juliet's boobs!" called the irritating male voice. Which kid was that, anyway? Maybe she should move him up closer. (As if she wanted the annoying child *closer* to her? Ugh.)

"I'll think about the movie," Summer said firmly. "What we *are* going to see is an art exhibit of Pre-Raphaelite paintings that features Ford Madox Brown's famous *Romeo and Juliet* balcony scene."

The classroom went dead silent. Finally a pleasantly plump redheaded girl who sat smack in the center of the class smiled up at Summer through extra-thick glasses and a face full of unfortunate zits and said, "You mean we're taking a field trip?"

"Yes, we're taking a field trip. Tomorrow."

There was a general class-wide sigh of relief and several high fives accompanied by murmurs of "Dude! That means no class tomorrow!"

"Okay, don't forget to work on the Shakespearian vocab I gave you at the beginning of class. It's due the day after tomorrow, and then we'll begin—" Summer was saying when—thank the blessed Goddess—the bell rang that signaled the end of the period as well as the end of the school day.

"High school sucks," Summer muttered to herself as the last pubescent boy filed out of her classroom, almost running into the door frame as he tried to keep his eyes on her cleavage as long as humanly possible. When the coast was clear, she dropped her head to her desk, and with a satisfying thud began to bang it not so softly. "I'm not a fool for teaching high school. I'm not a fool for teaching high school . . ." she spoke the litany in time to her head banging.

"Oh, honey. Just give up. We're all fools. That's one of the things that makes a truly great teacher: foolishness. The second thing starts with a *W*."

Summer looked up to see a tall, slender woman dressed all in black. Her acorn-colored hair was shoulder length and wavy in a disarrayed I'm-so-naughty style. She offered her hand to Summer with a smile just as the door to her classroom opened again.

"What?" The tall, slender woman whipped around, skewering the hapless teenage boy with her amber eyes.

The boy's eyes flitted from the scowling woman to Summer, and back to the scowler again.

"Mr. Rom? Isn't that your name?" asked the slender woman in a no-nonsense voice.

The boy nodded nervously.

"And what is it you wished to bother Miss Smith with?"

The boy's mouth opened, closed, and then opened again. "I have my journals to turn in. The ones that were due yesterday," he finally blurted.

The amber-eyed woman glanced down at Summer. "Do you take late work, Miss Smith?"

Summer swallowed. "No. I mean, isn't that the English Department's policy?"

"Of course it is." The slender woman raised one arched brow at the boy and trapped him with her sharp gaze. "No. Late.

Work. Means no late work. Now, go away, child, before you truly anger me."

"Y-yes ma'am!" the boy's voice broke as he backed hastily from the room and then scampered away.

"How in the world did you do that?" Summer said, gaping at the tall, young woman.

She smiled and held out her hand. "I'm Jenny Sullivan, your across-the-hall neighbor and fellow English teacher, as well as a Certified Discipline Nymph. Sorry, I would have introduced myself last week at the beginning of the semester, but I was on that delicious staff development trip to Santa Fe." Summer blinked blankly at her, so Jenny hurried on. "You know, Discipline in the Desert 101. Goddess! There are just so many applications for desert discipline in the high school class-room." She shook herself. "Anyhoodles, just got back today and heard that you'd taken your sister, Candy Cox's, place on our staff, and thought I better welcome you." She paused and glanced at the closing door after the student. "I see I arrived just in time."

"What's the thing that starts with a *W*?" Summer asked.

"Whips?" Jenny said hopefully.

"Whips? We can use whips here? Candy never told me that."

"Wait—wait. I think we're having a communication diffi-culty. You asked me for a *W* word and, naturally, I thought of whips."

"Okay, no. Let's start over. You said foolishness and something that starts with a *W* make us great teachers."

"Oh!" Jenny brightened. "Sadly, the answer to that is not *whips*, though it should be," she finished under her breath.

"Then it's . . ." Summer prompted.

"Whatever."

"Pardon?"

"The other thing. It's the Whatever Factor. Honey, I can already tell that your problem is you give a shit too much about what the hormones and germs are thinking."

"The hormones and germs?"

"Aka teenagers."

"Oh."

"Darling Summer, you need to understand that teenagers rarely think." Jenny patted her arm. "Come on, let's lock up, and then I'll treat you to a drink at Knight Caps."

Summer started to grab her keys and her purse, then her eyes flitted to the clock on the wall. "Uh, Jenny. It's barely three. Isn't that too early to drink?"

Jenny hooked her arm through Summer's and pulled her toward the door. "When you teach high school, it's never too early to drink. Plus, rumor has it you ate lunch in the vomitorium. You'll need a good healthy dose of martini to cleanse your system of those toxins."

"Vomitorium?" Summer asked as Jenny took her hand and led her toward the door.

"Just another word for the cafeteria. And, yes. You should be afraid. Very afraid."

"Wow. Teaching is so not like I imaged when I was in college."

"Darling, nothing is like you imaged in college. This is the real world." Jenny paused and then snorted. "Okay, well, Mysteria isn't actually part of the real world in the *real*ity sense, but you know what I mean. College is college. Work is work. Teaching is work."

Summer sipped her sour apple martini contemplatively. "Teenagers are a lot more disgusting than I thought they'd be."

"Preaching to the choir here," Jenny said.

"I mean, Candy told me to change my major to anything that didn't involve teaching, and I just thought she was, well . . ." she trailed off, obviously not wanting to speak badly about her sister.

"Here, let me help you. You thought Candy was just old, burned-out, and disgruntled. And that you, being twenty-some-odd years younger and ready to take on the world, would have an altogether different experience with *touching the future*." Jenny said the last three words with exaggerated drama while she clutched her bosom (with the hand that wasn't clutching her martini).

"Yeah, sadly, that's almost exactly what I thought."

<hr />

"Until your first day of real teaching?"

"Yep."

"And now you want to run shrieking for the hills?"

"Yep again."

Jenny laughed. "Don't worry. A few short lessons in discipline from an expert—that would be *moi*, by the by—and another martini or two, mixed with one of Hunter's excellent five-meat pizzas, which I'll split with you, will fix you right up."

"Okay, except I never have more than one martini, and, well, I'm a vegetarian."

"One martini? Sounds like you're a little tightly wrapped, girlfriend."

"I like to think of it as maintaining a healthy control."

Jenny rolled her amber eyes. "In my professional Discipline Nymph opinion, I might mention that 'healthy control' is often an oxymoron. And you're a vegetarian? Really?"

Summer chose to ignore Jenny's comment about control and said, "I'm really a vegetarian. I don't eat anything that had a face. Makes me want to throw up a little in the back of my throat even to think about it. So get my half with cheese and veggies."

"Cheese and veggies on your half it is." She motioned for one of the fairies to come take their order and then frowned when the pink-haired, scantily clad waitress ignored her and instead giggled musically at something a werewolf at the bar had said. Jenny lifted one perfectly manicured finger and started swirling it around in the air. "Looks like girlfriend over there needs a little discipline lesson. She needs to learn it's best not to ignore me when I—"

Summer grabbed Jenny's finger. "Do. Not. Use. Magic!"

Jenny yelped in surprise and put her finger away. "What gives?"

"Did Candy never mention what kind of, ur, *magic* I have?"

Jenny's frown deepened. "Well, no. Candy didn't have any magic, or at least she didn't until she hooked up with that handsome werewolf of hers. I think she felt kinda weird that everyone else had some sort of magic, so she didn't talk much about it. Plus, you know school's supposed to be a Magic Free Zone. There was no need to go into it much. Why? What's your magic?"

"Opposite."

"Huh?"

Summer sighed. "My magic is opposite magic. Any spell worked around me instantly turns opposite, or at the very least becomes totally messed-up and twisted around. That's another reason I decided to teach."

"To really fuck with the teenage mind by screwing up all the furtive little magics they attempt at school?"

"No, though that does sound like it might be a fun by-product. The truth is that I wanted to get a job back home in Mysteria. I really like it here. While I was in college, I missed . . ." She hesitated, trying to decide how much to say. "Ur, I uh, missed the people who live here," she finally decided on. And it was true. She had missed the people—some of them more than others. Actually, one of them more than others. "Anyway, I wanted to live in Mysteria, but I didn't want to constantly be messing up people's magic."

Jenny's expression said she knew there was more to the "Ur, I uh, missed the people who live here" nonsense, but the only comment she made was, "Oh, I get it. So working in the high school, a Magic Free Zone, sounded perfect."

"In theory," Summer said, mournfully sipping her martini.

"Hey, cheer up. It could be worse."

"How?"

"You could be teaching at the grade school. At that age they touch you *and* pee in their pants." Jenny shuddered. "Yeesh!"

Summer sighed. "This might fall under Emergency Procedures and require one more drink."

"Of course it does, and of course you do. I'll get it and order our pizza." Jenny slid her lithe body from their booth. "I'll go to the counter and order it. Although I do wonder what would happen if my kick-the-flirting-waitress-fairy-in-her-lazy-ass spell went opposite."

"You don't want to know. It's always a true mess and—"

A gale of giggles and the door opening caused Summer to lose her train of thought and glance over her shoulder at the entrance to the bar. Then she sucked air. Her face blanched white and then flushed a bright, painful pink.

"Oh, Goddess!" Summer whispered. "It's Kenneth."

✳ 2 ✳

"Yeah, it's Kenny the Fairy. So? What's the big deal?" Jenny was saying when the gaze of the tall, blond, male fairy in the middle of the new group of laughing girl fairies lighted on Summer and, smiling, he hurried over to their table.

"Hey, Summer! You're back!"

"Hi, Ken," Summer said, managing to stiffly return his hug. "Yeah. That's me. Back. For a week." And she blushed an even hotter shade of pink.

"Come on Kenny-benny! You promised to buy us mushroom pizza and those fizzy blue hypnotic drinks," pouted a pair of identical twin silver-haired, gold-winged fairies.

Kenny gave Summer an apologetic smile. "Sorry, gotta go. I'll call you later, okay? Is your number still the same?"

"Yeah. The same. Still." Summer tried to smile, but her face ended up looking more like an enthusiastic grimace.

"Oh, no no no. This is so damn sad. You have a crush on Fairy Kenny," Jenny said when they were alone again.

"Shhh!" Summer hushed her. "He might hear you."

"Oh, please. He's too busy with the slut sisters and their trampy friends. Hang on." Jenny turned, faced the counter, and nailed the giggling pink waitress with her stern gaze. Her voice carried easily across the bar, slicing through the chattering fairies like a saber through a butterfly-infested flower garden. "Esmeralda, we need another round of martinis and a veggie pizza. Now. And do not make me repeat myself." The waitress gulped, nodded, and scampered off to place their order. Jenny briskly brushed her hands against one another, as if pleased at a job well done, then she sat back in the booth, turning her full attention on Summer. "Okay, give. Why did you turn into the Incredible Cardboard Woman the instant Kenny-benny spoke to you?"

"I like him," Summer whispered, upending her martini and patting on the stem as she tried to coax the last of the liquid from the glass.

"Yeah, so? That doesn't explain the stiffness."

Summer sighed. "He and I grew up together. We were best friends, or at least we were until we hit puberty and I realized how gorgeous and perfect he is. Since then things have been kinda awkward between us."

"Kenny's been through puberty? Who knew?"

"Stop it! He's cute beyond belief. Don't you think he looks just like Legolas?" she said, shooting furtive glances at Ken.

"I guess so, only gayer. If that's possible." Jenny shrugged. "But whatever floats your boat."

"He definitely floats my boat," Summer said.

"Does he know that?"

"Huh?"

"You said you guys grew up together, and then things changed when you started crushing on him. Maybe you should let him know why things changed."

"Oh, I don't know about that. I'm not very good at—"

"Here are your drinks, ladies. Your pizza should be right out," gushed the waitress as she sloshed their new martinis down on the table in front of them.

"Thank you, Esmeralda. How kind of you to finally show us special attention."

"I—I just didn't realize it was you, Jenny," the fairy said. "Discipline Nymphs always get special attention at Knight Caps."

"As well they should," Jenny said smoothly, bowing her head in gracious acknowledgment of the fairy's apology.

The waitress hurried away, and Jenny turned her gaze back

IT'S IN HIS KISS . . .

to Summer. "So, you need to let Kenny know you have the hots for him."

"Ack!" Summer sputtered, mid–martini sip. She swallowed, coughed, and said, "Jenny, like I was saying, I'm not good at, well, the guy-girl thing. It's just so—I don't know—unpredictable."

"Oh, please. Kenny-benny isn't a guy. He's a fairy. And they're really predictable. They frolic—they flirt—they scamper."

"I happen to think there's more to Kenny than that, but as I said, I'm not good at the social interaction thing."

"You have issues with guys."

"No, just with guys I like."

"Okay, fine. Just with guys you like. What are you going to do about it?"

"Huh?"

Jenny snorted. "Darling, you're definitely old enough to take the bull by the horns. Figuratively and literally."

Summer took another drink of her martini. "You're right. I know you're right. But knowing and doing are two different things."

"Look, you don't seem especially tongue-tied right now. Actually, you've been rather amusing, so you're definitely not conversationally impaired. Just talk to the fairy."

"I'm only conversationally impaired when I have to talk to someone I want to sleep with. I like you, and you're attractive and all, but I definitely don't want to sleep with you."

Jenny preened. "Nice of you to notice I'm attractive." Then

her arched brows went up. "Hang on—you want to have hot, nasty sex with fairy boy?"

"No, I'd like him to make tender, slow, amazing love to me," Summer said, blushing again.

"Are you sure?" Jenny studied her carefully. "I'm getting the need-to-have-it-uncontrolled-and-hot-and-hard vibe from you, and I'm rarely wrong about my vibes."

"Jeesh, I'm sure. I don't do uncontrolled. Enough already."

"Okay, okay. You two are friends, right?"

"We were."

"You can still play off that. Hey, aren't you living in your sister's cabin at the edge of the woods?"

"Yeah."

"So, invite fairy boy over for dinner. You know," she winked, "for old time's sake. Then jump his bones," Jenny paused, rolled her eyes, and added, "slowly and tenderly."

Summer chewed her lip. "I don't know . . ."

"Take it from me. When dealing with men, fairy or otherwise, it's always best to be in charge and direct. Plus, you like control, and you'll definitely be in control if the date's on your turf."

"I'll think about it," Summer said, her eyes moving back to where Ken was perched in the middle of the group of fawning fairies at the bar.

"What you should think about is taking another gulp of that martini, putting on some of this nasty red lipstick, fluffing your hair, and marching yourself right over to that bar and extending the big invite to fairy boy." Jenny fished in her purse until she pulled out a tube of lipstick called Roaring Red and tossed it to Summer. Then she gave the giggling fairies a contemptuous glance. "You're cuter than those pastel pansies; don't let them intimidate you. Female fairies would lust after a snake if you put jeans on it and called it Bob. Everyone knows how easy they are, and no one takes them seriously."

"I guess I could." Summer gnawed her lip again. "I mean, we are old friends."

"Exactly."

She took a big drink of her martini, letting the alcohol burn through her body. Another gale of giggles erupted from the fairies, and Summer seemed to shrink in on herself. "I can't. I just can't. It's so . . . I don't know . . . *unplanned*."

"Girlfriend, life is unplanned. Get used to it. Okay, how about this deal: if you ask Kenny-benny over for dinner, I'll take my class on the field trip to the gallery with you tomorrow and be sure the hormones and germs act right."

Summer sat up straighter. "You'll come with me?"

Jenny shrugged. "I'm getting ready to start *Romeo and Juliet* with my freshmen, so I might as well. Plus, your students will probably behave dreadfully and need an ever-so-firm disciplinary hand," she finished with a gleeful smile.

"Promise?"

"That I'll jump squarely into your students' shit? Absolutely."

"Not that. Do you promise you'll come with me if I ask Ken out?"

"Yep."

"Even if he says no?"

"Don't put that negative energy out there. Of course he'll say yes, and of course, regardless of the fairy, I'll go with you tomorrow. Now gird yourself and go ask him out."

"Fine. Okay. I can do this." Summer gulped the last of the martini, ran her fingers through her curly blond hair, and in two quick swipes of Jenny's lipstick completed the transformation from Nice New Teacher into tipsy Discipline Nymph Trainee.

Just before she stood up, Jenny motioned for her to lean across the table. "Here, this will help." She deftly unbuttoned the top two buttons of Summer's blouse. "That's better. I'd do a quick make-your-nipples-hard spell, but what with your opposite magic, I'm afraid of what would happen."

"Don't even think about it," Summer said. She stood up and tossed back her hair.

"You are beautiful and powerful and desirable. Just keep telling yourself that."

"Okay. Okay. Okay." Nodding woodenly, Summer made her way to the bar.

"Kenny-benny, sweetie-weetie! You have a glob of cheese on your lip. Want me to get that for you, baby?" One of the twin fairies cooed.

"No, let me!" said her sister, using a tip of her wing to push her sibling out of her way so she could angle her lithe body closer to Ken.

"Girls, girls—settle! I can wipe my lip myself," Ken said, laughing.

"We know you can, honey-bunny!" said one twin.

"But it's so much more fun if we help you!" trilled the other twin.

None of them noticed Summer. At all. So she drew a deep breath, closed her eyes, and told herself, *When I speak, I'm going to pretend to be Jenny.* She opened her eyes, lowered her voice, and said, "Excuse me, I need a word with Ken." Summer almost jumped at the strong, stern tone she had (somehow) used. All of the fairies, including the ditzy waitress who was carrying their veggie pizza from the oven, turned to stare at her. *I'm Jenny . . . a Certified Discipline Nymph . . . beautiful . . . powerful . . . desirable . . .*

"Hi, Summer," Ken grinned at her. "Do you want me?"

"Y-yes, I do," Summer stumbled briefly, but then she straightened her spine and lifted her chin. "Could I speak with you? Privately?" She didn't let herself look at the scantily clad, beautiful fairies.

"Okeydokey!" Ken said. "Hang on, girls. I'll be right back." He took Summer's elbow and moved her to an unoccupied spot down the counter. "What's up?"

"Ken, I'd like to . . . um . . ." She swallowed the lump that had suddenly risen in her throat and made another attempt.

"What I mean is would you want to—" Thankfully, a fit of ridiculously loud coughing from Jenny interrupted Summer's babble and gave her a chance to pull herself together. "Ken, would you like to come over tomorrow night and have dinner with me?" she finally managed to say.

"Yeah, sounds cool. Are you living at your sister's cabin?"

"My sister's cabin. Yes."

"Great. So, I'll see you about eight?"

"About eight. Yes."

"Want me to bring something to drink?"

"Something to drink. Yes."

"Okay, see you tomorrow at eight!" He smiled again and went back to his seat at the bar.

"Okay. Yes. Yes. Okay," she told the air as she moved back to their table.

"Here, have the rest of my martini. You look shell-shocked. Are you okay? What did he say? How did it go?"

"Yes. He said yes," Summer said and then gulped Jenny's martini.

* 3 *

"Hangover. Ugh, I sooo have a hangover." Summer shakily sipped the sludge that almost passed for coffee she'd gotten from the teachers' lounge.

"I'm usually not a big proponent of control, but three martinis was probably one and a half too many," Jenny said. She studied Summer with a critical eye. "Good thing you're young. Only the very young can still look as good as you do this morning *and* deal with a wicked hangover."

"You keep talking like you're so much older than me, but you can't be over thirty," Summer said irritably.

"Oh, girlfriend, don't be silly. I'm two hundred and thirty-five. And a half."

Summer choked on her coffee.

"Discipline Nymphs are some of the most long-lived of the nymphs. It's because discipline is good for body and soul."

"I had no idea," Summer said.

"Well, girlfriend, you do now."

"Hey, speaking of stuff I'm confused about, would you please explain to me why a Certified Discipline Nymph is so roll-your-eyes about my control issues? Isn't control pretty much just another word for discipline?"

"Oh, my poor, deluded young friend. Let Ms. Sullivan help you. Discipline is what you have to be good at so you can release control. Girlfriend, you're too tightly wrapped. Flex those discipline muscles, relax that snoreable übercontrol you carry around with you, and you'll be amazed at the results."

"I dunno . . ." Summer said doubtfully. "But I can tell you I never thought of discipline as the antithesis of control before."

"Gives you a whole new outlook on discipline, doesn't it?"

"You're right about that. I can tell you that I'm going to start flexing my discipline muscles with the hormones and germs in my class. Like you said last night, I'm only going to call them by their last names, miss or mister whoever. It's much more formal; much more *disciplined.*"

"Well done, you!" Jenny smiled encouragement. "I knew you'd be a quick study. Speaking of the germs and hormones, let's round them up. I do believe I see the field trip bus waiting for us out there." As they herded the students onto the bus, Jenny called, "You did clear this with Barnabas, the gallery owner, didn't you?"

"I sent him an e-mail saying that I'd be bringing a busload of kids to view the exhibit today. I got a reply saying that would be fine."

"Good. I was worried for a second, because I thought I heard that Barnabas had left for a vacation to France. The nymph gossip said that the poor gay vampire took off to France because he was inconsolable about Hunter Knight falling for Evie Tawdry instead of him."

"But Hunter's not gay," Summer said as they followed the last student on the bus and took their seats near the front.

"Moxie, we've got them all," Jenny called to the short, squat, green-haired bus driver.

"Moving out, Ms. Sullivan," Moxie growled, let loose the emergency brake, and pulled the bus out onto the street.

"What is she?" Summer whispered. Eyes focused on the back of Moxie's green hair, she was sure she saw one of the thick strands move of its own accord.

"Mox? She's a troll. They make the best bus drivers. They don't put up with shit." And then, as if she literally had eyes in the back of her head, Moxie's head turned almost all the way around and she barked, "Sam Wheeler! Get your big, nasty boots off my bus seat. You are not at home. Put them up there again, and I'll take those feet off at the ankles. I'd much rather clean up blood than pig crap."

"Yes ma'am," Sam said sheepishly.

"See? Trolls know their discipline. Anyway, where were we? Oh yeah. No, Hunter's definitely *not* gay, as everyone, including Barnabas, knows. But I feel kinda sorry for the poor gay vamp anyway; unrequited love gets me right here." Jenny fisted her hand over her heart.

"Really? I wouldn't have pegged you for the sentimental type, Ms. Discipline."

"I'm not sentimental. I'm romantic."

"A discipline romantic?"

"Girlfriend, you have so much to learn. Romance is best with a healthy touch of discipline. Especially if it involves whips and handcuffs. And since we're on the romance subject, what's on the menu tonight with Kenny-benny?"

"I really wish you wouldn't call him that."

"Sorry. I'll be good. Promise."

Summer noted that Jenny's sparkly eyes said she was the opposite of sorry, but she decided not to say anything. Plus, she really did want to go over what she was going to cook for Ken. *She was going to cook for Ken!* Just the thought had her stomach rolling with nerves. She cleared her throat. "Okay, I thought I'd make a nice salad, with lots of lovely greens, and then have spaghetti with tofu and, of course, garlic bread, and maybe finish up with a big slice of peach cobbler. What do you think?"

"I think I was asking about your lingerie and not about dinner."

"But you asked me what was on the menu tonight."

"Yes, and I expected you to say something like, 'Why, Jenny, me and my lovely black panty and bra set are definitely the first three courses.'" At Summer's blank look, Jenny's eyes got big and round. "Oh, Goddess! When you asked him over for dinner, you *really* meant dinner."

Summer frowned. "Of course I did."

"Oh, um. Okay, well, tofu spaghetti sounds just dandy then."

Summer seemed not to have heard her. "Ohmygoddess! Do you think Ken thinks *I'm* on the menu, too?"

"Let's hope so," Jenny said.

"No!" Summer gasped. "That's not what—I mean, I wasn't thinking that. Exactly. Or at least not on our *first* date. That's isn't in accordance with my plan. We weren't going to have sex until the third date." She chewed her bottom lip. "Jenny, have I messed up?"

"Are you kidding? Kenny-ben—ur—I mean, Kenny isn't exactly Mr. Forceful. If he comes on to you, and you don't want to do him, just say no."

"I might want to do him," Summer whispered.

"Okay, then just say no nicely."

"But that wasn't what I was planning."

"Oh, please! Would you loosen up? If you want to have sex,

then boink the fairy. If you don't, then wait until the third or even the thirtieth date. Whatever."

Summer fanned herself. "I'm never going to be able to do this."

Jenny peered down her nose at her as if she were an unusual specimen under a magnifying glass. "Darling, didn't you date at all in college?"

Summer's cheeks flushed pink. "Yeah, of course I did."

"And?"

"And nothing. If I liked the guy, I decided when we'd, well, *do it*, and then we did it."

"Always according to your well-controlled plan," Jenny supplied.

"Always."

"Oh my Goddess! You've really never been swept off your feet by hot, sticky, steamy, raunchy sex."

When a couple of the kids sitting closest to the front of the bus gasped and laughed, Jenny turned her narrowed eyes on them, instantly quieting their tittering.

Summer frowned and lowered her voice. "No, and I don't think I'd like what you just described. It sounds so . . . so . . ."

"So out-of-control?"

"Yes. Exactly. And I'm not particularly good with out-of-control."

"That is shameful," Jenny said.

"Well, it's the way I am. And there's nothing wrong with the way I am," Summer said, more than a little defensively.

"Oh, girlfriend, I don't mean to make you feel bad about yourself. It's just that you're missing so much."

Summer shrugged. "I don't know. I had fun in college."

"I don't mean frat banging and one-night stands. I mean love."

"Huh?"

"Girlfriend, don't you know that love can't be controlled and planned and prepackaged or hermetically sealed to be taken out when it fits into your schedule?"

Summer chewed her lip and thought about Ken. When she spoke, her voice was so soft that Jenny had to tilt her head toward her to hear her. "I was kinda thinking that Ken would be the guy I let myself fall in love with. You know, college is over. He's here in my hometown. He's literally the boy next door."

"I don't know. It just sounds so clinical. And love is definitely not clinical." Jenny shook her head. "No. This will never do." She tapped a long, manicured red fingernail against her skintight black slacks. "What if I did a spell on you—one that I meant to be the opposite of what I really cast?" Before Summer could protest, she hurried on. "I could cast a control spell on you. That should get zapped by your opposite magic and allow you to relax with him tonight. Then what happens between you can at least happen naturally. Right?"

"Jenny, you can't ever, *ever* cast any kind of spell on me. It won't work like you expect. I guess the opposite magic isn't exactly the right way to describe what I have. It's more like opposite squared. It doesn't *just* make the spell reverse; it also makes it wacky."

"Define wacky."

"Okay, here's the perfect example. When I was in high school, Glory Tawdry thought she would help me out. It was right before our senior homecoming dance, and I didn't actually have a date with Ken, but I'd told him that I'd meet him there and would save all the best dances for him."

Jenny shook her head. "This has been going on between you two for years, hasn't it?"

"This?"

"Waffling. Unfulfilled romance. Missed opportunities. All because of your insane need for control."

"Yes. And my need for control is not insane. Anyway, as per usual for my high school days, overnight I grew the biggest, nastiest zit right in the middle of my forehead. No amount of makeup would cover it. It was like I had a third eye."

"Yuck."

"Yeah. So I asked Glory to cast a zit spell on me."

"Goddess! There's such a thing as a zit spell?"

Summer nodded. "She got the spell from her sister, Evie. You know she's a vengeance witch."

"Oh, that's right. Okay, go on."

"Well, it should have been simple enough. I wanted the zit gone. I have opposite magic. Glory casts a spell to fill my face with zits, which should have totally *cleared* my face of zits."

"It does sound simple enough."

"It didn't work out that way."

"What happened?"

"It cleared my face. Of everything."

"Everything?"

"Absolutely everything. I had no gigantic zit, but I also had no eyes, nose, or mouth."

"Shit! What did you do?"

"Freaked out. I knew it was bad, because I couldn't see anything, but when Glory started screaming, 'Oh great Goddess help! Her face is gone,' I lost it. I tried to scream with her, couldn't, so I did what any normal girl would do when scared shitless and utterly blind."

"You ran?"

"Yep. And promptly fell over my cool fuchsia beanbag chair, smacking my head on the corner of my very large and very metallic stereo cabinet, which negated the spell. Thank the Goddess."

"So your face came back?"

Summer nodded. "Along with the Cyclops zit. See, that's what happens when I think I'm smart, take a chance, and let my opposite magic do its thing. It never works exactly opposite. It's more like sideways, around-the-corner, upside-down magic.

And the spell only goes away if something major happens to me."

"Like smacking your head."

"Like smacking my head."

"Okay, I get that that was bad, and your control issues are making more and more sense, but have you ever tried to control your *magic* instead of controlling yourself?"

"Huh?"

"Think about it. You have weird magic, fine. Besides that, you have strong weird magic. How you've dealt with it is to clamp down major control over everything else in your life, but maybe all you have to do is to take control of your magic—you know, show it who's boss—and make it act right."

Summer shook her head. "You're nuts."

"I'm just sayin' discipline can be a good thing."

"Sure, for someone who is comfortable with it," Summer said.

"So get comfortable with it."

"Easier said than done."

"Maybe you just need the right incentive," Jenny said. "Want me to give you a quick dominatrix lesson or twelve? It'd be fun."

"Thanks, but no thanks. I think I'll just bumble along as I am, which means no 'helpful' magic spells from you or anyone else. Okay?"

Jenny held up her hand like she was taking an oath. "Promise." Then she added, "Guess it looks like you're going to have to get a handle on your übercontrol issues and your bizarre magic."

Summer sighed. "Sadly, it looks like it."

"Well, never fear. You have a Certified Discipline Nymph on your side. Plus, Kenny-benny may surprise both of us and take forceful control of your date tonight and ravish you properly." Jenny giggled and then, at Summer's frown, cleared her throat and sobered up. The bus lurched to an awkward halt in front of Dark Shadows, Mysteria's only art gallery. "But before anyone gets ravished, we will edify and educate the masses." She winked at Summer, stood up, smoothed her hair, and faced the bus full of teenagers. "Touch *anything* and you will have to deal with me—before school in the boy's restroom with a toothbrush, a can of Comet, and a collection of Shakespearian sonnets."

"What're the poems for?" whispered a voice from the silent, staring students.

"To clean your minds out while your hands—your *gloveless* hands—clean out the urinals," Jenny said sweetly. She turned around and, to a chorus of gagging sounds from the students, grinned at Summer. "Let's go, shall we?" Jenny sashayed from the bus, leading the way into the gallery with Summer and the well-disciplined students following close behind her.

Summer thought entering the gallery was like leaving one world for another. Inside the spacious building it was cool and dark. Even from the foyer she could see that instead of the usual plain white expanse of gallery walls, Dark Shadows had been painted in unyielding black, broken only by spotlights trained on each painting so that the entire exhibit gave the impression of floating dreams poised on the surface of a dark, sleeping sea.

"Wow, it's been years since I've been here, and I'd forgotten how dramatic the black walls make this place," Summer told Jenny in a hushed voice.

"Yeah, Barnabas told me that he hadn't planned the effect. He'd painted everything black only because it's easier on his vampire senses. The weirdness of it was just a happy by-product."

"Well, vampires gross me out with their definitely nonvegan diet, but there's something about this place that I like, even if it is a little creepy and—"

"Ladies, how may I help you?"

At the sound of the deep voice, Summer jumped guiltily and looked up . . . and up . . . and up into the face of a god of a man. He was standing just inside the shadowy entrance of the gallery, and even though it was dark and cool within, he was wearing mirrored sunglasses. As she blinked at her own reflection in those glasses, the man slowly reached up and removed them, revealing eyes so dark they looked black. His gaze locked with hers. *Gorgeous, dark, dangerous* were the descriptive words that flitted through her mind. "You're not Barnabas," she said abruptly.

One black brow lifted. "Astute observation, ma'am."

"Oooh, you must be Colin, Barnabas's older brother. Tell me I'm right, handsome," Jenny demanded, flipping her hair coquettishly.

"You're right." His eyes sparkled playfully when he turned to Jenny. "And you must be a Certified Discipline Nymph."

"Smart and handsome—my second-favorite combination," Jenny said.

"Your first favorite?" Colin asked with a sexy smile.

"Smart, handsome, and bound by the wrists," Jenny said.

Summer felt the urge to roll her eyes. Instead, she cleared her throat and said, "High school field trip—students—right behind us. Remember?"

Jenny shrugged, barely glancing at the wide-eyed students. "I'm just being friendly. But you're right. We should get down to business." The purr in her voice said that she'd rather go down on Colin than get down to any other business.

Summer frowned at Jenny and then stuck her hand out to Colin. "Hello, I'm Miss Smith. I sent the e-mail several days ago reserving the gallery for the field trip this morning. I'm assuming that's still okay, even though your brother isn't here?"

Colin took her hand in his, and Summer had to force herself not to gasp. His grip was strong, but she'd expected that. He was, after all, a *very* big man who had *very* big hands. It was the temperature of his skin that shocked her. Being touched by him was like being touched by an awakened statue. His hand was smooth, hard, and cool. Their eyes met again, and Summer was jolted by the dark intensity with which he was studying her—as if she was, at that moment, the most important thing in his universe. She'd only known of one species of Mysteria's

---

creatures who could spear someone with such intensity and whose skin felt like molded marble . . .

"You're a vampire!" she blurted, pulling her hand free of his firm grip.

His smile was slow and knowing, not in the least bit ruffled by her statement. "I am. Both of my brothers and I are vampires. It runs in the family, you know," he said smoothly.

"Does it?" Summer made herself not wipe her tingling palm down the side of her slacks.

"It does when you're all bitten by the same master vampire," he said.

Summer noticed that when he spoke to her, the playful sparkle that Jenny seemed to automatically evoke in his eyes changed . . . darkened, and even though he was no longer touching her, he was still studying her with that uncomfortable intensity. Feeling weirdly light-headed, Summer spoke more briskly than she'd intended. "That's interesting. Maybe we can talk about it later. Right now I think we should start our field trip. If that's okay with you—or your brother. Is Barnabas really not here?"

Colin cocked his head and looked down at her, a small curve of amusement shadowing his full lips. "Barnabas is in Paris drowning himself in wine and young Frenchmen so that he can forget being jilted by Hunter Knight." The vampire shrugged one of his broad shoulders. "Foolish of him to become so obsessed with a straight guy. I tried to tell Barnabas that Hunter's as gay as I am."

"Which is to say not at all," Jenny chimed in.

Colin's grin was almost a leer. He answered Jenny, but his eyes stayed on Summer. "Yes, ma'am. You're right about that."

"So, does that mean the field trip is off?" Summer said, wondering why Jenny's flirting with Colin should annoy her.

"Not at all. The reason I moved to town temporarily from my ranch is because Barnabas asked me to babysit this special exhibit. The field trip is definitely on. Besides, you just got here, Miss Smith. I'd hate for you to leave until we've gotten to know each other better." Colin's dark eyes trapped her gaze, and she felt her breathing deepen.

Is he making me dizzy? Is he working a vampire mojo on me? Summer mentally shook herself. She was being ridiculous. Magic didn't work on her. Or if it did, it went way wrong. Her overactive imagination and hormones were the only things working on her. What was probably happening was she was displacing her excitement about the impending dream date with Ken. No way was she interested in this vampire! He definitely didn't fit in with her well-thought-out plan for her future. "Excellent. Let's get started. The students have really been looking forward to this field trip," she lied.

"I hadn't been thinking much about this field trip at all." Colin lowered his voice so that it seemed to brush against Summer's skin. "At least not until I saw who was leading it. Now I do believe it's going to be a very interesting experience. It is good to meet you, Miss Smith." He tipped an imaginary hat to her in a cowboylike move that appeared to be second nature to him. Then he raised his voice so that the waiting students could hear. "Come on in and check out the art. And, yes, there are some nudes."

There were spontaneous high fives given in response as the students filed into the gallery.

"Ladies, if you'll follow me, I'll give you a more personal tour," Colin said. Though he spoke to both women, his eyes rested on Summer's face hungrily. He strode into the main gallery, giving Summer plenty of time to take in the faded jeans that snuggled his firm ass and the broad shoulders that strained the fabric of the black, long-sleeved shirt he wore. And were those cowboy boots? On a vampire? Sweet Goddess, gay Barnabas's brother was a sexy cowboy vampire!

"Damn, Summer! Are you secreting some kind of come-fuck-me! hormone? Tall, dark, and vampire is clearly hitting on you."

Summer pulled her eyes from Colin's muscular body and managed to scoff. "Oh, please. I'm so not interested in him."

"Really? That's not what your nipples are saying. Better check your control, girlfriend."

Horrified, Summer glanced down to see the outline of her very obviously aroused nipples pressing against her cream-colored blouse. Hastily she crossed her arms over her chest and muttered, "It's just cold in here," as she hurried into the gallery with Jenny's knowing laughter following her.

✳ 4 ✳

"All right! Move away from the nude, and no one gets hurt!" Jenny snapped, and the group of gawking teenage boys shuffled reluctantly away from the full frontal nudity of George Wilson's *The Spring Witch*.

Colin waited until the three of them were alone before saying, "Wilson was a big fan of Dante and William Blake, so he liked the poetic and romantic subject here."

Summer blinked in surprise up at Colin. The tall vampire actually seemed to know something about art.

"Huh!" Jenny snorted a little testily. "I don't see anything terribly romantic about witches. Sexy—maybe. Wanton—for sure. Romantic? Nah."

"The subject isn't a witch as we know them in Mysteria," Colin explained, his eyes on the nude painting. "It's actually Persephone as she emerges from the underworld. See the pomegranate in her hand?"

"Oh, well, that makes more sense. Goddesses are definitely romantic," Jenny admitted.

"What do you think of her, Miss Smith?"

Colin's question, as well as the intense gaze he shifted from the painting to her, caught Summer unaware, and she automatically said what was foremost in her mind. "I think I like her body better than most of the other women in the exhibit. They look too manly."

Colin's brows lifted. "I agree with you, Miss Smith. The Pre-Raphaelites tended to give their female models masculine characteristics. I like my woman to look like a woman, and not like a man in drag."

"As if that matters to the germs and hormones," Jenny said, eyes lighting on a group of laughing, jostling teenage boys clustered around the huge, colorful, and seminude painting of *Toilette of a Roman Lady*. "Excuse me for a sec. I'm going to kick some boy butt."

As she hurried toward the students, Summer called, "Herd them back into the main gallery in front of the Romeo and

Juliet painting. I'm going to give them their topic for the essay assignment."

Jenny's teeth flashed white as she grinned over her shoulder. "Oh, good. They'll hate that."

And, just like that, Summer and Colin were left completely alone for the first time.

She didn't have to look up at him to know his eyes were on her. Again. She could feel his gaze—against her skin, inside her blood. It heated her body, arousing her nipples and making her inner thighs tingle, and her woman's core became hot and wet and needy . . . needy for his touch, which wouldn't be sweet and gentle and loving, as she'd fantasized about Ken's touch being. Colin's touch would be like his body: hard and strong and sexy. No, Colin was nothing like Ken.

"What are you thinking about?"

His deep voice came from very close to her. *When had he stepped into her personal space?* She looked up at him. *Those eyes! They're so intense—so sexy.* He was close enough that his scent came to her, and it, too, was a surprise. Instead of smelling like the grave or worse, like a carnivorous, bloodsucking monster, Colin smelled as sexy as he looked. His scent was man mixed with something spicy, like cinnamon or even more exotic, like cloves and darkness and cool nighttime breezes sifting over love-dampened skin.

She stared at him and breathed the unique scent that was

Colin distilled by his own skin. *Nothing like Ken, who smells like lemons and laughter, and who I'm supposed to be having a dream date with tonight!* "My date tonight," Summer finally managed to answer.

Colin's dark eyes narrowed dangerously. "You shouldn't lie to me. You know vampires can smell lies."

Summer took a step back and put up her chin. She was damn sure not going to let this overbearing, way-too-masculine creature intimidate her, no matter how yummy he smelled. She was a college graduate and a professional teacher!

"Then you should sniff again. I was definitely thinking about Ken," Summer said with finality.

"Ken?" his dark-chocolate voice was heavy with amusement. "As in Barbie's boyfriend?"

"No. Ken, as in *my* boyfriend."

With a movement too fast to follow with her eyes, Colin grabbed both of her arms and lifted her so that he only had to bend a little to fit his face into the soft slope of her neck. He inhaled deeply and then let his breath out slowly, caressingly, so that it brushed against her sensitive skin and caused her to shiver.

"You may have been thinking, *briefly*, of him. But you do not have a boyfriend."

"What makes you say that?" she asked breathlessly.

"If you belonged to a man, I could scent him on you, and you smell only of yourself: sunlight and honey and woman."

He let her go as abruptly as he had grabbed her, and Summer stumbled back a couple of steps.

Her head was spinning, and her breath was coming short and hard. It was like he'd filled her mind with the white noise of the inside of seashells. All she could think to say was, "I smell like sunlight and honey?"

"Yes." Colin ran one cool finger down her heated cheek and the side of her neck. "Warm honey on a golden summer's day. You draw me to you like a field of lavender draws bees. Will you let me taste you?"

"Hey, Miss Smith! Miss Sullivan says we're all waiting for you, and we need you now. Uh, you better come, 'cause she seems kinda pissed."

Colin's hand fell away from her face, and Summer turned to see the little blonde cheerleader standing in the doorway to the main gallery.

"Y-yes. Okay. I'm coming. Now." Without looking back at Colin, Summer hurried from the room.

She could feel him following her. She thought it was like having a dangerous but darkly beautiful panther stalking her. He wanted to taste her! Summer shivered and crossed her arms concealingly over her breasts. Again.

"There you are, Miss Smith. The students are ready for their essay assignment." Jenny told her, then her eyes snapped over the group of milling students. "I said get your notebooks out. Now."

Book bags exploded as kids hurried to do her bidding. Summer could only watch in awe. How the hell did Jenny do that? She hadn't even raised her voice. Soon the entire room (which included one dark and brooding vampire) was looking expectantly up at her.

Summer cleared her throat. "The topic of your essay is this: a Pre-Raphaelite art critic wrote that this painting of Romeo and Juliet by Ford Madox Brown was 'splendid in expression and fullness of tone, and the whole picture is gorgeous in color.' I want you to be a modern art critic and tell me in your essay what you learned about Romeo and Juliet from Mr. Brown's painting." Summer paused, narrowed her eyes, and did what she hoped was a believable impression of Jenny's firmness, then added, "No, that does *not* mean that I want you to tell me Romeo is wearing a gay-looking red outfit, and Juliet's boobs are showing. What I want you to tell me is what this painting says about them as a couple. Questions?" She didn't give them time to ask any but hurried on. "Good. I'll let you have about fifteen more minutes here in front of the painting to take notes and start getting your ideas on paper."

A hand went up. It was one of Jenny's students, so she said, "What is it, Mr. Purdom?"

"Does your class have to write the essay, too?"

"Yes. I suggest you get busy," Jenny said smoothly.

There were a few muffled groans, but most of the kids settled down to studying the painting and taking notes.

"I'm going to go tell Moxie to bring the bus around. Do you think you can handle *it* by yourself?" Jenny's tone made the pronoun semi-suggestive. The sultry glance she sent Colin made it fully suggestive.

"Yes, definitely. No worries here," Summer said.

Jenny met her eyes before she left the room and blinked a couple times in surprise before her face practically exploded in a smile. "You like him!"

Summer felt her cheeks warm. "I don't like him. I don't even know him," she whispered.

"Okay, maybe I should have said you're hot for him. Well, go ahead, girlfriend. He's clearly more interested in you than me." She winked at Summer and disappeared out the front door.

Summer sighed and turned back to the room of sullenly writing students. Thankfully, Colin was on the far side of the room standing close to the painting. She could see that he was busy answering questions about it for some of the students. Good. That should keep him occupied. It also gave her an opportunity to study him. Goddess, he was handsome, but not in a typical fashion. What was he like? He reminded her of someone, and she couldn't quite—

Then, with a little jolt she did remember who he brought to mind. Her favorite fictional hero, Mr. Rochester from *Jane Eyre*. Yes, that dark, powerfully masculine look of Colin's would definitely fit in as master of Thornfield. *You know you*

IT'S IN HIS KISS . . .

think Rochester is the sexiest of all fictional heroes, as well as your favorite, her mind whispered. *No,* she told herself sternly, *Ken is really my type—all blond and sweet and gentle. He's what I planned for my future. The Rochester type needs to stay where he belongs—in the pages of fiction.*

But she was still staring when Colin looked up from the student he'd been helping and met her eyes.

Come to me . . . The words filled her—mind, body, and soul. Before she realized what she was doing, she was making her way around the group of students and heading for the vampire.

Summer was only a few feet from him when she stopped and shook her head, breaking the stare that had locked their eyes together and getting control of herself. Oh, hell no! What was she doing? Imagining his voice in her head and then obeying that imagining? Had she lost it? Had the stress of trying to teach teenagers cracked her already?

And then, not far behind her, she felt a too-familiar prickle up her spine. She knew even before she heard the whispered singsong words of the quickly uttered spell that one of the asshole teenage sorcerers-to-be had thought he'd be clever and whip up a little magic to see if he and his girlfriend could skip out of the assignment. Summer whirled around in time to hear the last stanza of the incantation. She opened her mouth to yell, *No! Stop!* Backing as quickly as she could away from the kids—and right into an impossibly hard, cold body she knew had to be Colin. She wanted to warn him. She wanted to do something—anything. But instead, the magic was already grabbing her, robbing her of speech.

Me and my bitch get in the picture, yo!
Somewhere our teacher can't go!
Where school and stupid essays ain't no mo'!
And it's cool to get with your ho!

Completely helpless, she did the only thing she could do. Summer closed her eyes, wrapped her arms around the pillar of strength that was Colin, and held her breath as she felt their bodies being wrenched, lifted, and tossed.

When everything was still again and the nauseating sensation of wobbly, opposite magic lifted, Summer slowly opened her eyes.

And looked straight into Colin's dark gaze.

"What the—" he began, and then his eyes widened in sudden fear. "The sunlight! I have to get out of . . ." The vampire's words trailed off as he realized he wasn't bursting into flame. Completely confused, Colin gazed down at Summer. "What's happened to us? It's day. I'm outside in the sunlight, and my skin is not burning."

"It's, well, because of my magic and that kid casting a spell. If I'm close enough to magic, it always messes up, and—" she began, and then her words broke off as what her eyes were seeing caught up with her mind. They were, indeed, outside. Actually, it wasn't full daylight, just a lovely morning dawning in the east. They were on a balcony, surrounded by a perfumed profusion of flowering rose vines. Colin was there with her, but he wasn't dressed in his jeans, black shirt, and cowboy boots. Here he was wearing an amazing crimson-colored outfit, rich as a king, or maybe even a god. She glanced down at her own clothes and gasped. She had changed, too, and was wearing only a soft, transparent chemise, which was cut low to expose her breasts to the nipples. She could feel Colin's eyes on those nipples as she looked up at him. "Uh-oh," she said. "I think we're inside the Romeo and Juliet painting."

✳ 5 ✳

"By the Goddess, I think you're right! How could this have happened?" Colin said, gazing around them while he shook his head in disbelief.

"It's me," Summer said miserably. "It's because of me that we're here."

His dark eyes rested on her. "How could this possibly be because of you?"

"It's my magic. Or maybe my nonmagic would be a better way to explain it." Summer sighed. "One of the students cast a spell in the gallery—something about getting inside the Romeo and Juliet painting so that he and his *ho*," she wrinkled her nose in distaste at the word, "could get out of the essay assignment."

"But what does that have to do with you? Other than it being your assignment?"

"I was close enough to the stupid teenager when he cast the spell to have my own magic work on it. And my own magic is opposite magic—kind of. Actually, it's more like sideways, opposite, totally screwed-up magic. The bottom line is that my magic messes up all other magic around me. So here"—she made a sweeping gesture, taking in the balcony and the pearly morning—"we are."

"In the Romeo and Juliet painting."

She nodded. "In the Romeo and Juliet painting." Summer smiled sheepishly. "Sorry."

Colin shook his head in amazement and lifted his hand so that the red velvet sleeve slid back to reveal his muscular arm all the way to mid-bicep. The morning light gilded his skin so that for that moment he looked tan and unexpectedly young.

"Incredible!" he said. Then he bared his other arm to the morning light, threw back his head, and laughed. "Do you know how long it's been since I've felt the sun on my skin?"

Summer couldn't answer him. She could only watch as he transformed from intense and brooding to vibrant and amazing. He laughed again and, with one swift motion, ripped open the buttons on his linen undershirt. Colin faced the rising sun, arms spread, face open. He'd been handsome before—all Rochester-like and mysterious. But here he'd transformed into a man whose beauty went beyond his height and hair and bone structure. This new Colin was so incredibly full of life that he seemed to vibrate with it.

"You did this?"

He turned the force of his full smile on her, and Summer thought that the heat he radiated would melt her. She nodded a little weakly and managed a "Yes."

With another laugh, he lifted her in his arms and spun her around the balcony. "I knew you were special from the moment I touched you."

"It's just my weird magic. I've been wishing I could figure out how to get rid of it or control it for years," Summer said a little breathlessly as he finally released her.

"Get rid of it? No way! And, take it from me, control is overrated. No! You're perfect just as you are—and so is your magic." He took her hand in his and, with dark eyes sparkling mischievously, he bent gallantly over it. "Thank you, my lady, for granting me a reprieve from unrelenting night and bringing me sunshine again."

Colin kissed her hand. As his lips met her skin, Summer felt a jolt of sensation that rushed through her body. His lips weren't the cool marble of a vampire! They were warm and soft and very, very much alive. She gasped, "You've really been changed. You're not a vampire here."

He didn't release her hand. Instead, he lifted it and slid it inside the open front of his shirt so that it rested over his heart. Summer could feel the beating of that heart under the warm, pliant skin of his chest.

"I don't know how long this magic will last, but I'm going to enjoy every moment of it."

"You're . . . you're so different here," Summer said, having difficulty concentrating on words with her hand pressed against his bare chest.

"Different?" Colin smiled and shrugged. "I suppose right now I am more like I used to be." He looked from her to the morning sky. "I think I've lived so long in darkness that I'd forgotten what it is to feel really alive." His eyes met hers again. They were full of the emotion reflected in the deepening of his voice. "You brought me the sun."

"On accident," Summer whispered. "I didn't really mean to."

"I smelled it on you when we met. Remember? I said you reminded me of sunlight and honey."

"I remember," Summer said softly, completely lost in his gaze.

"You drew me to you even then." He touched her cheek caressingly. "What is your first name?"

"Summer."

His smile was brilliant. "Summer! Perfect. Let me taste you, Summer. Let me breathe in your sunlight . . ."

Summer knew she shouldn't. She should step away from him and take control of this ridiculous situation and then fall on her head or whatever it took to break the spell. Instead, she felt her face tilt up to him as he bent to her lips. But he didn't kiss her—not at first. Instead, his mouth stopped just short of hers. She could feel his warm breath as he seemed to inhale her. Colin nuzzled her cheek and whispered into her parted lips, "You are sunlight and honey, *my* sunlight and honey."

Summer shivered. One of his hands still pressed hers against his chest. The other slid down her back, holding her close to him. She molded to him; only the transparent material of the thin chemise separated them, and she could clearly feel every part of his hard body.

"Do you want me to kiss you, Summer? Do you want me to taste you?" He breathed the words against her lips as he inhaled her scent.

"Yes," she whispered back. "Yes."

"Summer," he moaned, and then he claimed her mouth. His kiss wasn't gentle. It was rough and demanding. He possessed her lips, plundered her mouth, tantalized her tongue. His kiss engulfed her. It was the kind of kiss she'd always imagined she wouldn't like. It would be too filled with unbridled lust, too overwhelming and uncontrolled. So it was with a sense of utter surprise that Summer felt herself responding, body and soul, to Colin. She wrapped her arms around him and met his passion with her own. White-hot lust speared through her as the kiss deepened even more, as she gave herself completely over to him and—

IT'S IN HIS KISS . . .

—And Summer fell so hard on her butt that the wind was knocked out of her and she saw little speckles of light dance in front of her eyes.

"Thank the Goddess! You're back!" Jenny's hands were patting her as if she was checking for broken bones. "Are you okay? You had me so worried!"

Summer sucked air, blinked rapidly, and managed to nod.

"Is she hurt?" a deep voice asked.

"Colin? Oh, good. You're back, too," Jenny said briskly. "I think she's just had the wind knocked out of her. Here, help me get her to her feet."

Strong hands lifted her, and Summer realized that it felt familiar and somehow right that he was touching her again, even though his skin had lost the flush of sun-kissed warmth and was cool and marblelike again.

"Are you really all right?" Colin's voice came from close above her.

Summer looked up, finally blinking her vision clear. He was still holding one of her elbows, and he was watching her with the same dark intensity with which he'd studied her before they'd been magicked into the painting.

"I'm fine," Summer said. "At least I think I'm fine. I feel kinda—"

"Let's get you on the bus and back to school where the nurse can check you out," Jenny interrupted. "Colin, keep hold of her." And she marched off, leaving Colin to support Summer as they headed to the door.

Summer glanced up at the tall, silent vampire. He was Rochester again, with his broody expression and his dark intensity. Had it just been moments ago that he'd been laughing openly and so full of life and joy and passion? Especially passion.

"I'm sorry," she blurted, although she wasn't sure what it was she was apologizing for.

His gaze met hers as they came to the front door. "Don't apologize. I don't want to know you're sorry about what happened between us."

Summer frowned. Well, she was feeling dazed and confused, but she hadn't meant *that*. "No, I didn't mean—"

Jenny threw open the door, and a bright shaft of sunlight filled the entryway of the otherwise dark gallery. Colin dropped her arm and moved hastily back into the shadows, pulling his mirrored sunglasses from the pocket of his shirt and placing them on his nose so that he completed the metamorphosis from the charismatic man who had been seducing her on the balcony to the tall, silent vampire.

"Colin, I—"

"Come on. You still look terrible." Jenny's hand replaced Colin's on her arm, and the Discipline Nymph pulled her firmly from the gallery.

Over her shoulder, Summer could see Colin turning away as the door closed on the bright afternoon.

The kids were suspiciously quiet on the ride back to school. Jenny kept shooting them slit-eyed looks.

"Detention does not begin to describe what Mr. Purdom is going to be serving for a solid week," she muttered. Then her gaze shifted to Summer. "Do you think you're okay? You're still looking pale."

"I feel fine. I guess." She lowered her voice and tilted her head to Jenny's. "What did it look like to you?"

"Well, I was just coming back into the gallery when the girls were screaming bloody murder, saying you and Colin had disappeared. I was trying to figure out what had happened—by the by, Purdom and his buddy, McArter, were looking guilty as hell, so I knew the little turds had something to do with it—when that damn nosy girl . . . oh, what's her name? You know, blond, chubby, thinks she's way cuter than she is, and her mom's a witch with a *B*?"

"Whitney Hoge."

"Yeah, that's her."

"So Miss Hoge was pointing at the R and J painting with her mouth wide open, unattractively, mind you. I took one look at the picture, saw you two in place of the originals, and hustled the kids out of the room. I briefly chewed out Purdom's ass—will do a more thorough job of that later—and ran back into the gallery at about the time you landed on your butt in the middle of the floor."

"So no one watched us inside the painting?"

"Nope. No one was inside the gallery." Her brows went up. "Was there something to watch?"

"Sorta."

"Oooh! Nastiness?"

"Kinda."

"*Sorta* and *kinda* are not answers. They are especially not answers with details."

"I know," Summer said, and closed her mouth.

A sly expression made Jenny's face look decidedly nymph-like. "If I remember correctly, and I have an excellent memory—it's part of the whole discipline thing—anyway, if I remember correctly, you said that the way your opposite magic gets broken is by you being shocked. Right?"

"Right," Summer said reluctantly.

"Okay, then what shocked you so much the spell was broken?" Summer chewed her lip.

"Look, you can tell me. I'm a professional."

"A professional what?"

"Certified Discipline Nymph, of course. We wear many hats: classroom disciplinarian, workout disciplinarian—yes, I'm hell in the gym—and, most especially, *sexual* disciplinarian. So, give. Details, please."

"It was his kiss," Summer said.

Jenny blinked in surprise. "Colin's kiss shocked you so much that it broke the spell? Jeesh, was it that bad?"

"No," Summer said softly. "It was that good."

✳ 6 ✳

"No, Summer, I don't have your purse. Sorry. I'll bet you dropped it when that kid zapped you into the painting," Jenny said.

"Ah, shoot. I must have left it at the gallery."

"Could that have been a Freudian slip? Perhaps something that would give you a reason to see Colin again? You know you could just cancel the date with Kenny-benny, and go back there tonight," Jenny said.

"First, stop calling him that. Second, no, I'm not canceling my date. I'll go get my purse tomorrow or whatever. As I already explained, this thing with Colin was just a fluke. He's not my type, and he doesn't fit into my plan." A vision of Colin on the balcony, arms outstretched, head flung back, laughing his full, infectious laugh flashed through Summer's mind, but she quickly squelched the memory. That wasn't really Colin. The *real* Colin was much more subdued and uncomfortably intense, not lighthearted, fun, and happy. "The whole Rochester thing doesn't work for me in the real world," Summer blurted.

"Huh? Who's Rochester?"

Summer sighed. "You know, Jane Eyre's Rochester."

"Oooh! He's yummy. What about him?"

"That's who Colin reminds me of, and he is definitely not my type."

"You, my friend, might be insane."

"There's nothing insane about wanting a guy who's lighthearted and happy and fun. And blond," she added.

"You forgot 'and easy to control,'" Jenny added, then she hurried on, talking over Summer's sputtering protestations. "Girlfriend, just because a man is intense doesn't mean he's not happy and even fun sometimes, too. Plus, you might want to consider that lighthearted could mean light-*headed*, as in the guy might not have enough sense to be serious," Jenny said. "And what the hell's wrong with tall, *dark*, and handsome?"

"Not believing you about the whole broody-could-equal-happy thing," Summer said stubbornly, completely ignoring the obvious reference to Ken's brains or lack thereof. "And I happen to prefer blonds, light*hearted* blonds in particular."

"Did you prefer them when Colin had you in a lip-lock?"

"Yes. I still preferred them. I was just surprised, that's all."

"Which brings us back to my main point. You were surprised because it was so damn good. If it's so damn good, you might want to consider revisiting the scene of the crime."

"You want me to get back in the painting?"

"No, I want you to get back on the vampire."

"Jenny, I am going to get ready for my date. With Ken. The guy I'm really attracted to. So I'm going now. Bye."

"All right, all right! I hope you have a good time, and I want all the details."

"Good-bye, Jenny."

"Jeesh you're grumpy when you're sexually confused. Bye."

"I'm not sexually confused," Summer told the dead phone. She glanced at the clock. "Shoot! I am late, though." Putting Colin out of her mind, Summer rushed into the kitchen and threw the tofu spaghetti sauce together to simmer.

She also put Colin out of her mind while she showered. The warm water running down her naked body did *not* remind her of the warmth of his hands through the ultrathin material of the chemise.

"His hands aren't even warm. Not really," she muttered as she put on just a hint of makeup.

And she definitely didn't think about him while she picked out the ever-so-cute peach lace bra and panties set and then slid on the breezy, buttercup-colored skirt and the creamy, V-neck pullover that made her look and feel like a fresh spring wildflower, basking in the sunlight, just waiting to be plucked by a tall, dark—

"No!" she told herself, and marched into the kitchen. Summer was stirring the pot of sauce when the jaunty *shave and a haircut, two bits* knock sounded against her front door. She patted her hair and hurried through the living room.

"Hey, Sum! I couldn't figure out what kind of wine to get, so I got, like, three colors. I figured the more the merrier." Ken grinned boyishly and presented the bag that, sure enough, held a bottle of cheap Cabernet, cheap Chardonnay, and cheap white Zinfandel.

Summer returned his smile and motioned for him to come in, squelching her disappointment that there wasn't a bottle of nice Chianti in the mix. It wasn't like Ken could have known they were having spaghetti and that she preferred Italian wine with it. She'd just let him know next time. "How about we open the red? It'll go great with the spaghetti," she said.

"You made spaghetti?" He took off his jacket and dropped it over the back of the couch before she could ask him for it.

"Yeah, I hope you like it."

"Spaghetti's awesome! Hope it's almost ready. I'm starving."

P. C. CAST

She opened her mouth to tell him all she'd have to do is to boil the pasta, but he didn't give her a chance to speak.

"Hey, want me to come to the kitchen with you and open the wine? A drink would be awesome."

"Sure, come on back," she said and then led him to the back of the cabin and her sister's spacious kitchen.

"Wow, this is a great kitchen," Ken said appreciatively.

"Yeah, Candice loves her gourmet cooking." She sent Ken a shy look as she handed him the corkscrew. "Hope you're not disappointed that she got most of the cooking genes in our family."

"Nah, as long as it's hot and full of meat, I'm cool with it."

"Uh, Ken, didn't you remember that I'm a vegetarian?"

He looked up from opening the wine. "Huh? A what?" Then he glanced at the simmering pot on the stove. "Oh, you're worried I won't like your spaghetti." Grinning, he grabbed the big stirring spoon and ladled himself a generous taste test. "Yum! You don't have anything to be nervous about. This sauce is awesome!" he said through a full mouth.

"Oh, uh, good." Summer stirred the bubbling pasta. *What he doesn't know won't kill him,* she decided. Or at least she didn't think fairies were allergic to tofu.

While Summer put the finishing touches on their meal, Ken sat on her sister's pristine butcher block island, drank wine, and talked. And talked. And talked.

"Hey, Sum, so you actually made it through college."

"Yeah. It's funny—I didn't think I'd like the academic part of it, but once I got into my lit major I—"

"Man, I don't know how you stayed away from Mysteria for four whole years. No way would I want to do that. The mundane world is no place for fairies."

"Well, I did miss Mysteria, and, well, lots of the people here." She smiled and felt her cheeks get warm when she added, "Especially certain fairies. That's one of the reasons I came back."

"Of course you missed fairies. The world just isn't the same without them!" He jumped off the counter and bowed to her with a big flourish before pouring himself more wine.

He looked so boyish and carefree that she had to smile at him. "Then I should feed you so we can be sure you don't expire. I know how much fairies love food."

"That we do!" He hurried into the dining room where she had two places already set with intimate candles and her sister's beautiful china, leaving her to carry in the spaghetti and the sauce. He had thought to bring the bottle of wine with him, though.

So they ate, and Ken talked. And talked. And talked.

At first Summer just listened to him, commenting now and then (although his exuberant "conversation" really didn't require much participation on her part), and thinking about how cute he looked in the candlelight. His blond hair was thick and a little shaggy, but it looked good on him, and it glistened with a sparkle of fairy magic when the candlelight caught it just right. His blue eyes were big and expressive, his face completely animated. He really was a cute guy. And the direct opposite of dark and broody and intense and sexy . . .

No! Ken was sexy. She'd always thought he was sexy. After all, she'd had a major crush on him since they were teenagers. And she also—

"Sum, did you hear me? I said that you've really grown all up. It's kind of a surprise. Not that you don't look awesome," he hurried to add. "But it's a grown-up awesome. You've changed."

"Oh, uh, thanks. I think." Summer took a sip of wine. "You haven't changed at all," she said.

"Thanks, Sum! You know how fairies are—young for years. Good thing, too, 'cause the party planning and supply business isn't for the old and serious."

"So you're going into your family's business?"

"Of course! I love parties, and I especially love fireworks." He sat up straighter, clearly proud of himself. "You've been gone, so you probably don't know this, but I've been put in charge of the pyrotechnics for *Fairies 4 Fantastic Festivals, Inc.*"

"That's great, Ken. I'm really proud of you. Your dad must be—"

"Yeah, it's awesome! Just wait till you see what we're planning for Beltane this year. It's gonna be super cool with . . ."

Summer smiled and nodded while Ken talked. And talked. And talked. She also studied him. She hadn't been exaggerating. He really hadn't changed in the four years she'd been gone. He was wearing a T-shirt that said this way to the gun show with arrows pointing to his biceps. Summer had to stifle a giggle. His biceps were like the rest of his body, young and cute and lean. They were definitely not "guns," loaded or otherwise. And she definitely wasn't comparing them to Colin's muscular arms.

She mentally shook herself while Ken paused in his monologue to jog into the kitchen to snag the bottle of Chardonnay. He came back in the room, still talking about the plans for the "awesome" fireworks show that would be the climactic event of Mysteria's Beltane festival. She saw that his faded, baggy jeans were fashionably shredded over both knees, and he was wearing bright blue Skechers.

Nope, he definitely hadn't changed since high school.

It was about then that Summer began to wonder if dinner would ever end.

"Dang, Sum, sorry about your headache," Ken said as she handed him his jacket and walked him to the door.

"I guess I'm just tired from teaching all day."

He stopped at the door she'd opened and turned to face her. "It was great to see you again. I'm really glad you're back, Sum." Ken rested an arm over her shoulder nonchalantly as he slouched in the doorway. His blue eyes sparkled with another smile. "Dinner was totally—"

"Awesome?" She provided the word when he hesitated.

"Yeah, it really was. And you're awesome, too." Slowly, Ken bent to her. His kiss was sweet and questioning and very, very gentle. In other words, it was everything Summer believed she'd wanted in a kiss from the man she'd been fantasizing about for years.

She didn't feel a thing in response.

Give him a chance, she chided herself. *This is what you decided you want. He fits in the plan.* Summer leaned into Ken and put her arms around his neck, returning his questioning kiss with an exclamation mark.

She felt the surprise in his body, and then he parted his lips and followed her lead, kissing her deeper, longer. Summer thought he tasted, weirdly, like wine and lemonade. She wondered vaguely why he always reminded her of lemons—not the tart kind, but the supersweet Country Time Lemonade lemons, with lots of sugar. Lots.

Ken was still kissing her, softly and sweetly, while Summer's mind wandered. She was thinking about what she was supposed to teach her sophomores the next day as she absently looked over his shoulder at the dark edge of the forest. She thought she saw something move there, just inside the boundaries of her yard, and wondered what it was. The moon was high and insanely bright and almost about full. Could it be one of the town's many werewolves?

And then it hit her; she was thinking about school, and werewolves, and the moon while Ken was making out with her. That just couldn't be right. When Colin had kissed her, she hadn't been able to think of anything except him. His touch. His mouth. His taste. His kiss. Ken's kisses made her want to compile a shopping list or maybe fold some laundry.

No. This definitely was not going to work. Time to change the plan.

Instantly she pulled away from him. He gave her a sweet, boyish smile. "Sorry, Sum. Did I get carried away?"

"No, Ken, honey." Summer patted his cheek gently. "I got carried away. I think it's best if you and I stay good friends and don't mess that up with trying to be more than that. Do you know what I mean?"

Ken's smile didn't falter. "Sure, whatever. That's fine with me. Hey, do you think I could have some of that awesome spaghetti sauce to take with me so I could snack on it later?"

"Sure Kenny-benny," Summer said and, laughing, made him up a quick to-go package, patted him on his head, and said good night. Before she closed the door, she heard the distinctive giggles of several female fairies who had obviously been waiting to escort their Kenny-benny home. Or wherever.

She was still shaking her head at herself while she cleaned up the dinner dishes. "Jenny was right. I might be insane." Ken was so not the man for her. Actually, if she was being totally honest with herself, Kenny-benny was so not a man yet, and clearly, he might never be. Rinsing the dishes, she laughed out loud. She should be upset at having her fantasy of the Perfect Man blown to pieces and her future plan messed up, or at the very least she should have been disappointed, but she wasn't. She definitely wasn't.

Her hands slid through the warm, soapy water making her think of slick, naked skin sliding against slick, naked skin . . . of heat . . . and passion . . . and a kiss that could seem to stop the world . . .

No! She couldn't want the vampire.

And then, while washing Kenny-benny's very empty plate, she looked up at her reflection in the dark window above the sink. Her face was flushed, and her eyes were big and dark with desire.

"Am I absolutely positive that I can't want the vampire?" she asked herself.

Yes, you're absolutely positive, her reflection seemed to reply.

"But his kiss was—"

Reason one you can't want him, her refection interrupted, *is that he is a carnivore, and that makes you want to throw up a little in the back of your throat.*

"I don't have to eat what he eats. Oh, Goddess, I don't, do I?" Did one share one's blood with a vampire, or did one's vampire eat solo?

Reason two, her reflection continued, *his flesh is cold, dead, hard . . .*

"Well, what's wrong with hard?" she argued with herself. "Plus, he touched me before we were in the painting, and it really wasn't that bad."

Reason three, he's not your type!

"Okay, look," she told herself sternly. "Up until about ten minutes ago, I thought Kenny was my type. Maybe I need to change my type!"

Reason four—her conscience ignored her—*he makes you feel out of control, and you don't like feeling out of control.*

"Well, that's because he was unexpected. He's expected now, so I won't have a control problem. I left my purse at his gallery." Silently she thanked the Goddess for that slip, Freudian or not. "I have to see him one more time."

"Yeah, so, tomorrow I'll just swing by the gallery after school and pick up my purse," she talked around her toothbrush to her reflection in the bathroom mirror. "No big deal. No enormous ulterior motive," she lied. "Just getting my purse, saying a quick hello, then coming home. There won't be any more kissing. None at all. It wouldn't even be appropriate. Really."

Summer crawled into bed, thinking about the difference between Ken's kisses and Colin's kisses. *What a difference . . .*

Why had she ever thought passion and heat were bad

things? Okay, she knew the answer to that, even if she didn't like to admit it. She was scared of too much passion, that it would cause her to lose control, and if she lost control, she'd get burned. Summer had learned that lesson well with her stupid out-of-control magic. Maybe it was smart of her to be scared. Was playing with a vampire like playing with fire? Or ice?

Fire, she decided as her body heated the cool sheets. Colin's passion had been exactly like fire. Her hands touched her lips, remembering Colin's caress, and then slid slowly down her body, pausing to cup her breasts. Her nipples ached. Summer squeezed them, gently at first, and then she craved more, and her touch got rougher as she teased her ultrasensitive nipples. She moaned. Almost as if she couldn't stop the impulse, one of her hands moved down between her legs. Summer gasped at the slick heat she found there. She was liquid with desire. She closed her eyes and stroked herself. As her orgasm built, Summer imagined hands on her body and lips against her skin, and when her release came, it was Colin's intensity that she was thinking of and his touch she yearned for.

✳ 7 ✳

Colin had never felt like such an utter fool. What in all the levels of the underworld was he doing walking through the moonlit forest carrying a purse? *I know exactly what I'm doing. I'm being a gentleman*, he thought. *I may be dead, but chivalry isn't. Summer left her purse at the gallery, and I'm returning it.* A woman's purse was a sacred thing. Goddess knows what all was kept in one; Colin would almost rather take a long walk outside at noon than actually look in the damned thing. Thankfully, it was zipped closed, but he still held it gingerly, like it might explode if he handed it too roughly. There wasn't much he could do except return it. The sooner the better. Sure, he could hang on to it and wait for Summer to realize where she left it and then come claim it. But she'd been through a lot. It might take her a day or two, hell, even three, to get around to it. Until then, what about all that important stuff inside the purse? The only thing he could do with a clear conscience, was to return it to her right away. Or at least that's how he rationalized his overwhelming need to see her again—immediately.

The package carefully wrapped in the gallery's chic, black, hand-pressed paper was a damn sight tougher to rationalize away.

Or maybe not. Colin shrugged his broad shoulders. Why hide behind rationalizations? He was courting a woman. That was nothing to feel foolish about, even if it meant carrying her purse through the woods while pink love petals fell from the sky and fairies giggled annoyingly as they played naked hide-and-seek among the trees. Goddess, fairies were irritating!

Colin glared at a silver-winged, pink-haired fairy who had frolicked close to him and given the vampire a coquettish smile that was a clear come-hither invitation.

"Not interested," he said firmly, giving the naked creature a dark look.

Not at all offended, she shrugged her smooth shoulders and scampered off.

Colin scowled after her. Fairies had never interested him. Actually, now that he was thinking about it, it had been a long time since any woman had caught his interest. Were he completely honest with himself, he would admit that no woman had affected him as this one had. And it wasn't simply because she was beautiful and interesting. Summer had brought him sunlight!

Summer . . . Colin felt the urge to laugh aloud. The name fit her perfectly. Sure, he knew she'd said the whole sunlight thing had been because of how her magic worked on spells, but she'd been wrong. He'd smelled sunlight on her, felt it in her touch, since the moment he'd taken her hand.

After living in darkness for so long, there was one thing he definitely recognized, and that was the touch of the sun. He had to have more of that touch. So he was going to woo her until he won her.

"You're so different here," she'd said of him on the balcony, and she'd seemed to like the difference. Colin had been different. He'd been himself again—or at least his prevampire self. Unending night had worn on him until he'd become as dark as his surroundings. Even his ranch had become a black place for him. He'd never been able to go out on his land, work his horses, or care for the cattle in the daylight. He hired hands to do that for him. But for decades he'd found solace in roaming his land at night—in chasing the last rays of sunlight as day reluctantly gave way to night, and then, in turn, giving way to the sun as it inevitably reclaimed the sky. Not so recently. Recently his life had seemed nothing but unending darkness, his beloved ranch not freedom and open space, but just another gilded cage where night continued to imprison him.

Living a life of shadows had worn on him and darkened Colin's personality as well. But that wasn't really *him*. It was what this damn vampire curse had turned him into. Summer could change that; Summer could change everything, and he wanted her to. He wanted to be the Colin who laughed and lived and loved again.

So he'd put in an overseas call to his brother who was still sleeping his way around gay Paris, and Barnabas had told him Summer was staying in her sister, Candice's, cabin, which sat in a clearing at the southern edge of the pine forest surrounding Mysteria. Which is why he had just trekked through said forest with Summer's purse and a gift for her and why he was now standing just inside the edge of trees facing the brightly lit little cabin with its homey, wraparound porch.

Colin drew a deep breath. Sunlight and honey—he could scent her from there. She had to be home. He started forward, telling himself that the jittery feeling in his stomach wasn't nerves, it was just anticipation. Which was only natural; it had been decades since he'd been interested enough to actually consider courting a lady. He just needed to remember that he used to be good with the ladies. Charming—that's how they used to describe him. Out of practice he may be, but he'd dig deep and put back on that old charm, and Summer would see that—

The door to her cabin opened, and Colin came to an abrupt halt when a man's body was silhouetted clearly in the doorway. Summer joined the guy, and Colin's gaze focused on her, blocking out the man and the night and everything but this amazing woman who was, to him, a waking dream.

He loved what she was wearing. The skirt was soft and feminine, and coupled with the creamy yellow of her shirt and the gold of her hair, she looked just like she smelled: like a vision of sunlight and sweetness. He wanted to take her in his arms and mold her softness to his body and inhale her fragrance until he had to fight with himself not to explode.

Then the guy moved, blocking his view of Summer. With a growing sense of horror, Colin watched the jerk nonchalantly drape an arm over her shoulder. Another scent came to him then: one of lemons and laughter and . . . and . . . fairies?

The asshole who was trying to steal his sunshine was a fairy? His jaw tightened, and it felt like someone had slammed a sledgehammer into his gut when the Goddess-be-damned fairy bent and began gently kissing Summer. For a moment Colin stood, rooted into place. Then, with a small sound of disgust, he turned and melted back into the darkness of the forest.

Just beyond vision of the cabin, Colin paced . . . and paced . . . and paced. He had the urge to throw her purse into the branches of the nearest pine and break the carefully wrapped package into a million little pieces, but he managed to control himself, although just barely.

Summer had said she had a boyfriend, but he'd scented her then and hadn't smelled even a hint of another male on her. He had most definitely *not* smelled that fucking blond lemon drop! Yet the fairy had been there—in her home—with his lips all over her.

IT'S IN HIS KISS . . .

All right. Fine. He should have expected a woman as attractive as Summer to have other suitors. He would just have to step up his game. He was more than a match for the lemon drop. Fairies, even the wingless male variety, were all fickle sluts. Didn't Summer know that? Maybe she didn't. His brother had said she'd just moved back after being away for most of her four years of college. Maybe she didn't have much experience with adult male fairies. Colin's jaw clenched again, and his hands fisted. He'd crush that damn lemon drop into a little yellow speck if he did anything to hurt her.

By the time he'd paced off his temper and returned to Summer's cabin, the lights had been turned out. The scent of lemon fairy had also been extinguished, which helped to calm him. The damn lemon drop hadn't stayed the night. Colin left his offering on the porch just before dawn.

The morning was gorgeous. It was weird how getting rid of an old crush had cleared her vision. Her plan had been flawed, but that didn't mean she shouldn't get busy on a new one . . . a new one that might just be tall and dark and handsome. She really shouldn't obsess so much about being in perfect control. And, anyway, she could handle the vampire. She'd certainly handled the fairy. She was definitely interested in Colin, or at least she thought she might be interested in him. Well, she was going to stop by the gallery on her way home from school to get her purse. She'd see then if there really was any attraction going on with the vamp and take it from there.

Summer felt amazingly alive and happy as she slathered black raspberry jam on a piece of toast and munched on it hurrying out of the cabin on her way to school—and almost tripped and fell face-first over the heap of stuff in front of her door.

"What the—" Summer rubbed the knee she'd landed on, looking back at the pile of . . . "My purse," she murmured. Sure enough, her purse was there. Right in front of the door. Sitting next to it was a package wrapped in expensive black tissue paper. There was a simple ivory card taped to it that just said *For Summer* in an old-fashioned-looking cursive script. Intrigued, she fingered the card and then opened the package carefully, so she didn't mess up the beautiful paper.

Summer gasped and oohed in pleasure. It was a copy of the Romeo and Juliet painting, reproduced in oil on canvas and framed in an exquisite gold-painted wood frame.

"Colin," she whispered and felt a thrill of pleasure thrum through her at the sound of his name.

"That might be the most romantic thing I've ever heard," Jenny said over the barely edible lunch they'd bought from the vomitorium, aka the school cafeteria.

"It has to have come from him. Right?"

Jenny rolled her eyes. "Of course it came from him. Hello!

IT'S IN HIS KISS . . .

He brought back your purse, and—now, correct me if I'm wrong, but I do believe he's the only vampire you got zapped into the R and J painting with."

"Definitely the only one."

"The vamp is wooing you," Jenny said smugly.

"Wooing? Is that even still a word?"

"Yes. And that's what he's doing. So prepare yourself."

"For what?"

Jenny shook her head sadly. "Oh, you poor child. I would imagine that a rough ballpark on your vampire's age is probably at least two hundred."

Summer blinked. "He's not my vampire."

"Yet," Jenny said.

"Two hundred," Summer said as if she hadn't spoken. "As in years old?"

"Yep."

"Wow."

"And as that very tasteful, expensive, and sexy gift shows, men used to know how to do some wooing."

"Wow." Summer considered Jenny's words as she tried to chew her soyburger. "I'm going over there," she said decisively.

"To the gallery?"

"Yes. I'm going to thank him for the painting. And for returning my purse. Plus, uh, I'd, well, like to make sure there's no misunderstanding about anything he might have accidentally seen last night."

"You lost me on that one."

"Ken kissed me good night last night."

"So? You said you decided you're totally not interested in him."

"I did, and it was his kiss that sealed my decision. But first I thought I should give him a chance, which meant I kissed him back."

"Again, so?"

"Well, I was kissing him and looking over his shoulder and thinking about the moon and lesson plans and stuff, and I thought I saw something—or someone—outside by the edge of the woods. Then the next morning I found my purse and the painting on my front porch."

"Wait, back up. Kenny was kissing you, and you were thinking about lesson plans and crap like that?"

Summer nodded.

"That's a damn shame. I don't know what the hell's wrong with fairies these days. Kenny-benny doesn't ring my bell, but damn! He's a *fairy*, a fey being who practically has sex and frolics for a living. He should be able to hold a woman's attention with a kiss."

"Don't be so hard on him. I'd just been kissed by Colin, and the comparison was not good for Kenny."

Jenny rolled her eyes. "Yet you were going on and on about how you weren't interested in the vamp and how he wasn't your type and how he didn't fit into your control-freak plan."

"I'm not a control freak, or at least not all the time. Anyway,

Colin might not be exactly what I've thought of as my type, but he's definitely a better kisser than Ken."

"Big surprise there," Jenny said.

"Be nice," Summer said.

Jenny rolled her eyes again.

"Like I said, I'm going to swing by the gallery after school. This time it'll be just me and not a busload of germs and hormones. Maybe sparks will fly again between us, maybe not. But I'm going to give him a shot."

"Good idea. And speaking of germs and hormones, I'm not done deciding on that damn Purdom kid's detention for that bullshit spell he cast yesterday. I'm still looking into the he-had-an-accomplice angle."

"You might want to interrogate McArter; they're buds. Oh, and remember, don't tell him about my magic," Summer added quickly.

"I got it the first hundred times you told me to keep quiet about it. Don't worry; I think it's hilarious that they don't know about your magic. Makes them think their magic is totally screwed up, which serves them right. They shouldn't be using magic at school or at a school event. Brats," Jenny said, eyes flashing.

The bell rang, and both women sighed. "Back into the fray," Jenny said.

"Do you think it's possible to Shakespeare freshmen to death?" Summer asked.

"One can only hope," Jenny said.

* 8 *

Summer checked her lipstick in her car's rearview mirror and smoothed her hair, feeling insanely thankful that the day was bright and clear and humidity-free, which meant she was having a good hair day. She glanced at the front of *Dark Shadows*. There were no other cars parked close by, and she mentally crossed her fingers that three o'clock was too early for evening visitors and too late for lunchtime visitors, so it would be empty. Well, except for Colin, that is.

She could do this. She could go inside and smile and thank him for returning her purse and leaving such a great gift. She could figure out a way to let him know that Kenny was history.

And maybe, just maybe, she could see if that amazing sizzle that sparked between them yesterday was more than just a magical fluke. Then she could consider revising her future plan to include him.

Before she could chicken out, Summer forced herself to get out of the car and enter the dark, cool gallery.

Her first thought was that her hunch had been right; the gallery appeared deserted. Her second thought was that it was very uncomfortable to be standing there all by herself with only the feeling of being watched to keep her company.

The feeling of being watched?

Definitely. She definitely could feel eyes on her: dark, hungry, intense eyes. Almost as if he drew her gaze, she turned her head and looked deeper into the shadows of the gallery. Sure enough, Colin was standing there, his gaze locked on her.

"Good afternoon, Summer," he said.

His voice reminded her of dark chocolate and wine and sex.

"Hi," she blurted, hating how nervous she sounded. Then she cleared her throat and got control of herself. "I hope you don't mind me just dropping in like this."

His lips tilted up slightly. "It's a gallery. The idea is for people to drop in."

"Then I'm glad I have the right idea," she said, tilting her own lips up.

"And I'm glad you came by. I wanted to see you again. Would you like to come back to my office?"

"Yes, yes, I would."

Summer's smile increased as she followed Colin, getting another excellent view of his tight butt as he led her through the room with the Romeo and Juliet painting, back to an inconspicuous door that opened to an ornate, fussily decorated office.

"This is definitely not you," she said, running her finger down the back of a gilded Louis the Something-or-Other chair. Then her gaze flew up to him as she tried to gauge if she'd just offended him.

He simply shrugged and said, "You're right. This is Barnabas's office, and it's definitely him. He likes pomp and circumstance and lots of gold."

"And what do you like?" Summer heard her voice asking the question that had flitted automatically through her mind. She clamped her mouth shut. She usually had more control than speaking her thoughts aloud, but she found herself being temporarily glad of her lack of control when his gaze went dark and intense as he answered her.

"If you mean what kind of decoration, I like it more masculine, although I don't think a house is really a home without a woman's touch." The vampire blinked, obviously surprised at his response, and then he smiled almost shyly at Summer. "I think that's the first time I've admitted that to myself."

"Admitted that you like a woman's touch?" she asked softly.

His gaze trapped hers. "Admitted that I *need* a woman's

touch," he said. "But I shouldn't be surprised. You affect me oddly, Summer."

"Is that a good or a bad thing?" she asked.

"For me, it is a very good thing," he said.

They stared at each other until Summer became uncomfortable under the heat of his scrutiny. "Thank you for returning my purse to me," she said, trying to temper the electricity that was building between them with words. "And I absolutely love the Romeo and Juliet painting. Thank you for it."

"I'm glad you like it. I wanted to give you something that might make you remember what happened yesterday."

"It's been kinda hard for me to forget," Summer said.

"For me, too." Colin moved closer to her. "Yesterday meant a lot to me. I haven't felt the sun on my skin in many decades. It's not something I want to forget."

"You know I didn't do it on purpose. I can't bring you the sun again." Summer was finding it hard to think rationally with him so close, but her mind was working enough that she wanted to make it perfectly clear to him that she couldn't just zap them back into the picture; she couldn't make the sun shine for him.

Colin touched the side of her face. "You're wrong about that."

Summer shivered. His touch was cool, but her skin beneath his fingers came alive with heat.

You are my sunshine.

Summer jumped when his voice sounded inside her head.

"You heard that, didn't you?" he said.

"Yes," she whispered. "I also heard you call to me from across the room yesterday."

That dark intensity was back in his eyes, and he spoke with such emotion, such passion, that Summer's heartbeat quickened, and she felt her breathing deepen.

"You don't know me, and I don't know you, but there is something between us that I've not experienced until I touched you yesterday. You say you can't bring me sunshine again, yet to me your skin, your breath, your hair, even the summer-sky color of your eyes—all of you is light and shining to me. It is as if, somehow, magically, you are literally *my* summer, *my* sunlight."

"I—I don't know how that could be. I'm just me." Summer couldn't help leaning her cheek into his hand. His scent and touch were intoxicating, and she wanted nothing more at that instant than to get closer to him.

"I don't know how it could be either, but you are an unexpected gift that I plan to cherish. If you'll let me. Will you give me a chance, Summer?" Colin lifted her chin. "I realize I'm not what you're used to—not the kind of man you would consider a *boyfriend*." He ground the word out. "And yesterday you said you were already seeing someone."

"I'm not," she said.

IT'S IN HIS KISS . . .

"Not?"

"Not seeing anyone." She stared up into his dark eyes, utterly mesmerized by his closeness.

"But last night . . ."

"Was nothing. There's nothing between us. Ken isn't my boyfriend."

"I saw—" he began.

"You saw him kissing me. It was just, well, basically a test. I wanted to see if he could make me feel what you made me feel."

"And did he?"

"No," Summer said, staring into the vampire's eyes. "Not even maybe. That's one of the reasons I'm here. I had to see if it was still there," she said softly.

"It?"

"The sizzle between us."

Colin smiled. "It's still there. Let me taste you, sunshine, and I'll prove it to you."

"Yes," she whispered, already leaning into him.

Colin didn't claim her mouth right away. Instead, he drank in her scent and touch, mingling breath with breath. "I want you more than you can know." He spoke the words against her skin. "When I touch you I'm alive again. I can feel the sunlight on my face." He nuzzled her neck and then buried his hand in her thick blonde hair and breathed in the scent of sunlight and honey that clung to her.

"Kiss me, Colin," she murmured.

With a strangled sound, his mouth finally met hers, easily erasing any lingering memory of Ken's soft, sweet, boring kisses. His skin didn't have the heat it had the day before, but it didn't matter. It was still *him*, and Summer craved his taste and touch like she'd never wanted anyone or anything before in her life.

When they finally broke apart, it was only to stare dazedly at each other. "What is it between us?" Summer said. "It's crazy. It's like you're my human version of catnip."

His smile took away what was left of her breath. "I'm your catnip; you're my sunshine. I think we make an excellent pair."

"But I don't even know you. You're practically a stranger."

Colin took her hand, threading his cool fingers through her warm ones. "Can you say we're strangers when we're touching?"

Summer looked down at their linked hands. His was so pale and large and strong, and hers was tan from working in her sister's flower beds. They seemed direct opposites. He was the opposite of everything she'd believed she wanted for so many years. Yet he was right; when they touched, something was there, and it was something that hadn't been there with any man before him.

"Colin, we have to slow down. I have to think about—"

The buzzer that signaled the opening of the front door of the gallery made both of them jump. Colin threw a dark look over his shoulder. "I'll get rid of them and close the gallery; then we can talk." Like an amazing old-time gentleman, he kissed her hand before he started out of the room, but he stopped in the doorway, glancing back at her. "You were right, Summer. You don't really know me, and I don't know you. But what I do know is there is something special between us. I've walked this earth longer than you—a couple hundred and some odd years longer." She gaped at him. Was everyone a zillion years older than her? Colin's smile was sad and his eyes haunted with loneliness as he continued. "I can promise you that in all the long years of my life I haven't ever felt what I do when I so much as breathe in the scent of your skin. If you feel even a fraction of what I feel, how can you not give us a chance?"

"What if this is all just because of my messed-up magic?" she asked.

"What if it isn't?" Colin said.

Then he turned and left the room.

Summer's knees felt wobbly, and she dropped down into the closest gilded chair. What was going on with them? One thing was sure; the attraction between them was still there, in spades! She wiped a shaky hand over her brow. He was right. She'd never felt anything like what Colin made her feel just with the touch of his hand on her face, let alone his lips against hers. What would happen if their naked bodies pressed together? A thrill of anticipation sang through her. Could she handle such passion, and if she couldn't, what happened then? Was it worth taking a chance on? What was it the ancient Greek playwright,

Euripides, said about too much passion . . . something about a lion loose in a cattle pen?

Plus, she really didn't want to be in love with a vampire. Besides the whole vegetarian/carnivore issue there was the day/night issue. She loved daylight and sunshine and all that went with it. Wouldn't she have to give that up to be with Colin?

Her head was starting to ache when the voices that had been drifting to her from the outer gallery began to register.

"Yeah, man, we didn't mean for nothin' bad to happen," said one male voice.

"For real. We were gonna come by today and say sorry, even if Ms. Sullivan hadn't made us," added another.

Summer snorted a little laugh. That had to be Purdom and one of his partners in crime. Jenny had been right. There was more power behind that spell than one kid could have conjured.

"That Ms. Sullivan is one mean woman," said the first voice.

Summer smiled. Yep, Jenny had definitely known it.

"Yeah, but she's so fiiine," said the second, she now recognized as her student and Purdom's bud, Blake McArter.

She heard Colin's deep voice answering them but couldn't quite make out what he was saying. She attempted to sit still for a minute more, then curiosity killed discretion, and she walked quietly to the doorway of the office.

"We thought we'd make up a little thang for ya," said Purdom.

"Like, to make up for what we did," said McArter. "Okay with you if we bust out with it?"

"Sounds fine with me," Colin said.

This time she could hear Colin's voice more clearly, and the good humor in his tone made her smile. Her feet seemed to move of their own accord as she continued walking soundlessly down the hall. After all, she'd been a victim of Purdom's magical stunt. He should apologize to her, too. Well, again, that is. Naturally, Jenny had made him grovel appropriately at school earlier that day. But still, more groveling never hurt, plus the other kid was here, too, this time. She crept slowly into the gallery until she came to the room that held the Romeo and Juliet painting, aka the scene of the crime. The two boys were standing in front of the painting with their backs to her. Colin was facing them, so he could have spotted her, but his attention was focused, with an amused lift of one of his dark brows, on the boys as they started making the ridiculous rap noises that always reminded Summer of a mixture of farts and messed-up engine sounds. As McArter did the sound effects, Purdon rapped their song.

> We come to apologize 'bout the other day.
> See, we didn't know you and Miss S. would go away.
> We was just tryin' to get in some play.
> We sorry you had ta dress all gay.
> And then Miss S. and you almost went all the way.

Those brats! They did know Colin and I had been in the painting! At that point there was a "musical" interlude in the rap, and both boys mouth farted and popped around looking silly and semicharming at the same time. Summer had just decided she'd been entertained enough and had started forward again when her eyes went to Colin, and she froze in place. He was watching the boys and laughing with the youthful joy of a man filled with light and promise. And Summer once again saw the happy, open man who had shared the painting, and his passion, with her.

He was completely and utterly captivating.

It was then that the question of whether she should risk getting entangled in a life of passion and darkness became moot. She *was* entangled with him already. Somehow within this dark, brooding vampire there lay the man she'd fantasized about and longed for all these years. It wasn't a question of fitting him into her future. Colin was her future.

Summer must have made an involuntary sound, because Colin's gaze instantly went from the boys to her. The smile didn't leave his face; on the contrary, when their eyes met, his joy seemed to blaze from him to her.

"So we be here to make yestaday okay," rapped Purdom.

"Yea, we got to give you somethin' 'cause Sullivan says we got to pay," intoned McArter.

"And she's scary—even though I'd like to tap that play."

The fart noises came to a crescendo, then Purdom went into the closing lines of the rap.

IT'S IN HIS KISS . . .

"We thought 'bout what we could do that would stay.

"And come up with a magic spell to melt our dissin' ya away."

Magic spell? Those words broke through the smoldering look she was sharing with Colin at the same time she noticed that the little shivers going up and down her spine weren't just because she was hot for the vampire. *The rap was really a spell the boys were casting!* Then four things happened simultaneously.

Summer opened her mouth to scream at the kids to stop.

Colin moved toward her with an inhuman speed that blurred his body.

Purdom finished the rap/spell with the line, "Dude, we give you a future bright as the sun's ray!"

And as the vampire's body slammed into Summer, she realized the magic catastrophe was unavoidable, so she closed her eyes and braced herself, sending out one concentrated desire: *This will not mess up Colin and me.* Then the area around her exploded with light.

* 9 *

When Summer opened her eyes, she was in a strange bed in a room she didn't recognize. It was nice—she noticed that right away. Actually, it was freakishly like her dream room: huge, antique iron bed piled with rich linens in soft blues and yellows. The furniture was simply carved oak, well made and expensive but not fussy. The floor was glossy pine wood, dotted here and there with thick butter-colored area rugs. The walls told her she was in a log cabin—a damn big one at that. There was a fireplace along one wall. The others held several incredible original watercolor paintings of landscapes that all had one thing in common: they were bright and beautiful and painted in the full flush of summer days.

Then her eyes caught something on top of the long, low dresser. Was that her jewelry box? She climbed down from the mountain of a bed and realized two things: One, she was wearing her favorite style of pajamas: men's boxer shorts and a little matching tank top. Two, it was, indeed, her jewelry box sitting on top of the dresser. Actually, as she looked around the room more carefully, she saw that the jewelry box was just one of several items that belonged to her. Over the ornate beveled mirror hung one of her favorite scarves. The Kresley Cole book she'd been reading was on the nightstand beside the bed, as was her favorite honeydew-scented candle. Feeling surreal and very *Twilight Zone*–ish she opened the top drawer of the nearest dresser and, sure enough, inside was a neat row of her bras and panties.

"What the hell is going on?" she cried, and then, wondering how she could have been stupid enough to forget, memory flashed back to her, and she recalled the two boys and their rap that had become a spell and the terrible light that exploded just as Colin had grabbed her.

Light? Colin?

Light! Colin! The two definitely didn't mix. Where was she, and where was Colin? Summer hurried to the window and peeked out. The sun was setting into the mountains, painting the lovely landscape around the cabin in hues of evening. She was definitely in a cabin, out in the woods. But it wasn't her sister's cabin. She tried to calm her freaked-out mind. *Think—I have to think! The kids' spell finished with something about Colin having a bright future. Goddess! Did that mean he was trapped in the dark somewhere? And if so, why was she here in this pretty cabin?* It didn't make one bit of sense.

"Okay. Okay. You're a college graduate. You can figure this out," she told herself. "This room looks like it could belong to you, so . . ." With sudden inspiration, Summer went back to the bedside table and, sure enough, plugged into the charger, just as it was in the bedroom in her sister's cabin, was Summer's cell phone. She grabbed it and dialed the first number that came to mind.

"Summer! Where are you? Are you okay?" Jenny's voice was uncharacteristically frantic.

"I'm fine, I think, and I don't know where the hell I am. Where's Colin? Is he okay?"

"Other than having lost his damn mind worrying about you, your vamp's fine. And what do you mean you don't know where you are?"

"What do you mean he's lost his mind?" Summer and Jenny spoke their questions together.

"I can't tell—" Summer began.

"He's freaked completely—" Jenny said.

Both women paused. "You start," Jenny said. "Why don't you know where you are?"

"'Cause I've never been here before. I'm at a gorgeous cabin and, weirdly enough, it's not just decorated exactly how I would

---

IT'S IN HIS KISS . . .

have decorated it, but a bunch of my stuff's here. Now tell me what's up with Colin."

There was some unintelligible noise in the background and then Jenny said, "I'll do better than that. I'll let Colin tell you himself."

Summer could hear her passing off the phone, and then Colin's deep voice was in her ear. "Summer? Are you hurt? Where are you?"

"Colin! Are you okay? What happened?"

"I'm fine; don't worry about me. Are you okay?" he said.

"Other than not understanding what happened, I'm fine. Especially now that I know you're okay."

"I am okay, Sunshine." She could hear the smile in his voice. "Now that I'm not scared into my second death. Don't ever disappear like that on me again."

"Disappear? Is that what happened? All I remember is a bright light. Are you sure you're okay? I know the whole light thing isn't good for you."

"I didn't see a light. The kid finished the spell just as I grabbed you, and then an instant later my arms were empty, and you were nowhere." His voice lowered. "I don't like my arms being empty of you."

His words made warm, fluttering things happen in the pit of her stomach. "Yeah, I know," she said.

"Where are you? The sun's setting. I'll come to you."

"I wish you could. I don't have any idea where I am. I woke

up in this beautiful iron bed in an amazing room that, weirdly, has a bunch of my stuff in it." Summer walked to the bedroom door while she kept talking. "I peeked out the window, and I'm somewhere in the mountains—great view, by the by—in a big cabin. You should see this place. Your brother would definitely appreciate the quality of the watercolors on the walls, and they're all of summer landscapes. I haven't gone out into the rest of the house yet, though."

"Does the bedroom have a large, wood burning fireplace in it?"

Summer nodded. "Yeah, it does."

"Go out into the rest of the cabin, and tell me what you see." His voice had a strangely excited tone to it.

"What's going on, Colin?"

"I have a hunch. Just leave the bedroom, and I'll know if I'm right."

She took a deep breath and opened the door. "Okay, this is definitely my dream home," Summer said.

"Describe it to me, Sunshine," Colin said.

"I'm on a landing looking down at an incredible living room. The furniture is all leather, but it's not too testosteroney because it's mixed with antique end tables and thick, furry rugs. Oh, Goddess! I hope it's fake fur."

Colin's deep laugh was in her ear. "I'll bet it is now."

"Now? What do you mean?"

"First, go down the stairs and into the living room and describe to me the painting over the fireplace."

"Okay, it's kinda freaking me out that you know this place."

"Don't be scared, Sunshine. Trust me. All will be well."

She loved the tone of happy excitement that filled his voice and hurried down the stairs. Sure enough, there was a huge painting over the fireplace, and when Summer realized what it was, she laughed aloud. "It's the Romeo and Juliet! Goddess, it looks like it's the original."

"It is, sweet Sunshine. Stay right where you are; I will come to you."

"You know where I am?"

"I do, indeed. You're home, Summer."

"You're home, Summer" was all that Colin would say before he hung up. What did that mean? But she didn't have time to worry and wonder, because all of a sudden a dark mist began to spill into the room. Wordlessly, Summer watched it surround her and thicken and then change, elongate, and solidify until Colin was standing in front of her.

He looked around them, and his handsome face blazed with a triumphant smile. "I knew it! Makes me really glad I didn't eviscerate those boys."

"Colin, would you please explain to me what's happened?"

"*We've* happened," he said, still smiling. "This"—he swept his arm around them in a smooth motion—"is my home. Only it's been changed. A woman's touch has been added. *You've* been added to my home, Summer."

Summer stared around her in amazement. "This is your home?"

"It is."

"How did this happen?"

"The boy said that he was giving me a bright future. His spell, mixed with your magic, has gifted me with you." Colin closed the space between them and took her in his arms, inhaling her scent and touch. "Let me show you how much we belong together."

"Colin." She spoke his name like a prayer and reached up to touch his face. The instant her hand met his cheek, the vampire gasped and jerked as if she'd zapped him with a jolt of electricity. Summer pulled back, afraid she'd hurt him, but what was reflected in his dark eyes wasn't pain, but wonder.

"Touch me again, Summer."

Before she could respond, Colin took her hand and pressed it back against his cheek, and this time Summer saw the glow of light that came from her hand and felt what was happening beneath her palm. The vampire's cool flesh shivered and then flushed and warmed.

"What's happened?" she whispered.

"You're bringing light to me again, my darling. Only this time your magic is calling alive my flesh." He turned his face so that his lips pressed against the palm of her hand. She felt a tingle of heat pass through her hand, and then his lips were on

IT'S IN HIS KISS . . .

hers. They were warm and insistent and very much alive. Speaking only her name, Colin lifted her into his arms and strode from the living room up the stairs, kicking open the bedroom door and gently placing her on the bed.

When he bent to kiss her again, she pressed him gently away from her. "Wait, I have to see . . . I have to touch you and know . . ." she murmured.

Slowly, carefully, she unbuttoned his shirt, pulling it apart so his muscular chest was bared to her. Then she lifted her hands and, pressing her palms against his skin, began at his shoulders, sliding her hands down his chest in a slow, thorough caress that spread light down his body. Against her glowing skin his flesh warmed, and she watched in awe as his carved marble skin and muscles shivered and then, as long as she touched him, flushed with health and life. When her hand reached the place over his heart, Colin moaned—a sound part pain, part pleasure—and he pressed his hand over hers, stilling her caress.

"Ah, Goddess!" Colin said. "My heart beats again!"

"I can feel it. Oh, Colin! I can feel it beating."

"Don't stop touching me, Summer. Don't ever stop touching me."

Light-headed with the swirling emotions of passion and awe and desire, Summer looked into Colin's dark eyes and saw love and life and her future there. And then she closed her eyes and bowed her head, breathing deeply while she tried to calm her turbulent emotions. *I will not lose control and cause this to end! I will not!*

* 10 *

"Summer, what is it?" Colin's voice was filled with worry.

She opened her eyes and met his gaze. "I'll never stop touching you, Colin. I promise, but you have to let me be with you on my own terms."

His expression only became more confused, and mixed with that confusion Summer saw hurt and withdrawal. "I know that my being a vampire is hard for you. I understand you might not want to bind yourself to someone like me."

"No, no I didn't mean that," she explained quickly. "It has to do with my magic. I have to maintain control of my emotions, because if they surge too much and I lose control, the spell will be broken and the messed-up magic, along with all of this, will end."

"Sunshine, *this* isn't as simple as a spell or magic. What's happening between us is real."

"I hope so," she said. And then she drew her hand down his arm again, watching as the glow under her palm warmed his cool flesh. "But *this* is definitely magic, and I don't want this to end for you."

"As long as I have you, I'll have sunlight—magic or no."

"You have me, Colin," she said, but still Summer controlled her breathing and kept a firm hold on her emotions as, never taking her hands from his skin, she undressed him. First she pushed off his shirt, skimming her hands down his arms until she threaded her fingers through his, staring into his eyes as her touch brought his skin alive.

"Summer," he moaned her name. "I never imagined I could feel like this again."

"How do you feel, Colin?" Summer asked breathlessly as her mouth moved down his naked chest.

"Like a man, Sunshine. You make me feel like a man again."

His words sent a thrill through her body. Summer caressed Colin's waist, reveling in her ability to give him such pleasure. She unzipped his jeans, and he stepped out of them. She stared at his naked body and imaged that she knew what Pygmalion felt as his sculpture of Galatea came to life.

Calm and slow, Summer reminded herself as she pulled him

down beside her on the bed. *Focus on giving him pleasure.* When his eager hands reached for her, she allowed Colin to pull her into his arms. Her mouth met his as she pressed her body against his nakedness. Separated by only the thin cotton of her boxers and tank, it was an exquisite sensation to feel her heat warming him, her flesh bringing him alive.

His hardness pressed low and insistent against the softness of her stomach, and while their tongues met her hips shifted, bringing him fully against her core. He moaned against her mouth as she thrust against him, sliding him the length of her wetness.

When her head started to spin, she broke the kiss. Concentrating on controlling her breathing and trying to find calmness within her again, she rolled over on top of Colin and held his wrists, stilling his roving hands, which had been kneading her aching breasts. "Let *me* touch *you*," she said, regaining her breath. When he started to protest, she stilled his words with a kiss, then whispered against his mouth, "I don't want the magic to go away, Colin. Help me keep the magic."

"Sunshine, I've been trying to tell you that you *are* the magic." His voice was deep and rich with desire.

"Humor me," Summer said with a smile and then began to move down his body, kissing and caressing. When she reached his cock, she took him in both of her hands, loving the textures of him, the hardness sheathed in such soft skin. Still stroking him, she glanced up and met his gaze. "You're wrong, Colin.

It's you who's magic." And then she bent and let her tongue flick out around the engorged head of his cock. He moaned her name as she licked the length of his shaft, discovering how exciting it was to be able to bring him such intense pleasure so easily.

"Do you want me to take you in my mouth?" she asked huskily.

"Oh, Goddess, yes!" he gasped.

Summer swallowed him. He was too large for her to take all of him in her mouth, but she stroked his shaft with her hand, squeezing while she tasted him, loving how his cock heated and pulsed beneath her touch. She cupped his heavy testicles, and another moan was torn from his throat as his hips lifted to give her better access to him.

"Your body is so beautiful," she murmured against his skin, teasing the head of his cock with her tongue. "I never knew a man's body could be so beautiful."

Then she swallowed him again. "Summer!" Colin gasped her name, his voice rough with barely controlled lust. "I can't stand much more. If you don't stop, I'm going to come in your mouth."

Summer loved that *she* was evoking this response in him. She felt gorgeous and sexy and very much in control. "Then give in to it," she purred, imagining for the first time in her life that she was the Marilyn Monroe type, the kind of woman men dreamed about. "Give in to me." She laved his engorged head with her tongue while she ran her hands down his thighs, feeling his muscles tremble and warm under her hands.

Summer heard a ripping sound as his hands gripped the thick comforter while he struggled to maintain control, and then he moved with a vampire's preternatural swiftness, and suddenly his hands were lifting her, and she was on her back looking up at him.

"Colin, wait, I need to do this my way!"

"Sunshine, lovemaking is something best done together, rather than controlled by one. And I have to have my turn." She started to protest again, but the dark intensity of his gaze caught her. "Trust me, Summer. Trust that I'm telling you the truth when I say that what's happening between us is more than an accident of magic."

"I trust you," she said softly, *but I'm still going to stay in control,* she added silently to herself.

His smile had a sexy, feral glint as, with one flick of his powerful hands, he ripped the cotton tank off her. Colin cupped her breasts, running his thumb lightly over her already sensitized nipples. She gasped and bit her bottom lip.

"Since I saw these beautiful nipples, aroused and pressing against that sweet teacher's blouse you had on yesterday, I've thought about doing this over and over again." His head dipped down, and he took her nipple into his mouth, sucking and licking gently. She threaded her fingers through his thick, dark hair and pressed him more firmly against her. "Harder," she

IT'S IN HIS KISS . . .

whispered, and then all her breath left her body in a rush as he went from gentle to forceful, pulling on the nipple with his teeth while he lifted his hard thigh between her legs so that her hips could lift and grind against him.

Control . . . control . . . she reminded herself frantically. Summer breathed deeply, letting the pleasure wash in waves over her but not allowing herself to drown in it.

Colin shifted his attention to her other breast, and she closed her eyes, feeling the desire that was building inside of her but keeping it banked just enough that it didn't engulf her.

Then his mouth followed the edge of her rib cage down to the soft indentation of her waist. He hooked his fingers in her shorts and quickly skimmed them down her body, leaving her naked before him. She felt a moment of embarrassment, but it passed when she saw the expression on his face and heard his husky, "Sunshine, you're even more exquisite than I dreamed you would be." He kissed her stomach reverently, gently, before letting his hands glide down her body to cup her buttocks. He positioned himself between her legs as he lifted her to his mouth.

Summer stopped breathing completely when his tongue parted her folds and dipped within.

"You taste just like you smell: like sunlight and honey," he murmured against her intimately.

When his tongue found her clit, her hips buckled against

him. She squeezed her eyes closed, fighting against the cascade of pleasure. She wanted too badly to let loose, to allow him to make her come against his mouth. But what would happen then? How could she bear it if she was suddenly transported, midorgasm, back to her cabin—alone?

"Colin, come here to me," she said, reaching to pull him up to her. When he only intensified his caresses, she added, "I have to feel you inside me."

That got through to him, and he raised himself over her. She took him in her hand again, lifting her hips so that she could position the throbbing head of his cock against her wet opening. Summer was already getting her breathing back under control, and she'd keep that control while he spent himself inside her—at least she hoped she could. That Colin could turn her on was abundantly apparent, but being turned on and actually orgasming were two very different things.

This would be for Colin. She'd bring him light and life and love. She'd let him bring her to completion another time, when she was sure her emotions wouldn't cause their whole world to disappear. So her plan was to take him inside her and just maintain her sanity this once. She'd worry about next time the next time. Everything would work out in the future when she—

"Look at me, Summer."

His voice brought her attention back to the present. She looked up into his expressive, dark eyes.

"I want to look into your eyes while I love you, while I make you mine," he said. He thrust into her with one powerful plunge, filling her completely.

Summer gasped as the pleasure spiked through her. Her hips lifted to meet his as her legs wrapped around him. Colin braced himself on one arm, raising up so that he could continue to look into her eyes. The vampire impaled her. They moved together, slick and hot.

Summer felt her body gathering itself, and she fought against it, even though the pleasure was so intense that it bordered on pain. But she maintained control—she did it. Until Colin reached between them and began rubbing his thumb rhythmically against her swollen, slick clit.

"Colin!" she gasped. "Oh, Goddess, I can't—"

"Shhh," he whispered. "What we have is beyond magic. If you trust me, give yourself completely to me. I can prove it to you. Will you trust me?"

"Yes," she said without hesitation. "I trust you, Colin."

"Then I make you mine, truly and completely." He bent his head to her neck. Summer felt his lips, his tongue, and finally his teeth. At first they just grazed her, then she felt him gather himself, and Colin bit her, puncturing through the soft skin above her pulsing vein.

The pleasure she felt at his claiming was as sharp as the bite, and she couldn't fight against her desire any longer. Summer felt the wave begin within her and knew it would utterly, completely overwhelm her. She grasped Colin's shoulders and, for once in her life, completely gave up control to a man, body and soul. As her body shuddered in orgasm, and he joined her in release, she felt the familiar tingle of her magic becoming active. This time instead of running, or bracing herself against it, or fighting it, Summer released her magic, instead choosing to hold on to Colin and his promise that there was more between them than smoke and mirrors.

The flash of light against her closed lids had Summer opening her eyes in surprise. Colin jerked back from her neck as if her blood suddenly burned. And then *he* was burning as the light that had been focused in Summer's hands surged from her into him.

"Colin!" Summer cried, trying to pull away from him, trying to stop the transfer of light.

"Trust me, Sunshine," Colin ground the words out between teeth clenched in pain. "I accept any price I have to pay to be with you, and it will not separate us." At his words the light intensified until it bowed his body. The vampire screamed, and then he was knocked from the bed. He landed on the floor, limp and unconscious.

Summer was sobbing when she rushed to him, touching his face, calling his name, praying to the Goddess to please let him wake up . . . please, she'd do anything . . . just please . . . please . . .

Colin drew a deep breath and then exhaled, coughing pain-

IT'S IN HIS KISS . . .

fully. Summer helped him sit up. "Colin! Goddess, are you okay?"

"I'm fine." His voice was raw, as if he hadn't spoken in centuries. "I'm fine," he repeated, after clearing his throat. He started to take her in his arms but suddenly froze. "Blessed Goddess!" He sounded utterly shocked.

"What is it? Maybe I should call someone. A vampire doctor?"

Then Colin completely surprised Summer by jumping to his feet, throwing back his head, and laughing with uninhibited joy.

Still on the floor, Summer looked up at him, utterly confused. "Colin?" Was he hysterical? Is this how vampires acted when they'd been mortally wounded?

"I don't need a vampire doctor, Summer, my sunshine, my dream, my love. Somehow, someway, you and your magic have made me human again!"

She stared at him, this time really seeing him. He was still a tall, handsome man, but the marble cast of his skin was gone. It had been replaced by the healthy flush of a living, breathing man.

And she wasn't touching him at all. He was truly alive.

"It'll go away," she whispered. "It won't last."

"I think you're wrong, Sunshine," he said, pulling her to her feet. "Have you ever given up trying to control your magic before tonight?"

"No," she said slowly. "I've always fought it or run from it.

And it's not just my magic I gave up control of tonight, Colin. It's my life. When I trusted you, I had to give up being in total control of myself."

"I think there was something about your decision to trust me that drastically affected your magic." Colin cupped her face. "All these years you've believed your magic was flawed, messed up. I don't think it was. I think it was pure light—the pure energy of sunshine—and when you gave me your complete trust, when you relinquished control, you also gave your magic to me."

"It should have killed you. You're a vampire; you can't stand the light."

"Perhaps, but I've never loved the light until I loved you. I desired it, coveted it, yearned for it, but never really loved it until you."

"So my light didn't kill you."

"No, Sunshine. Your light burned away the darkness of my past and saved me."

"So now you think we can make love and I can orgasm without worrying about us being zapped apart."

"Over and over again, Sunshine," he said, smiling.

"Sounds like a perfect happily ever after to me."

"Me, too, Sunshine. Me, too."

Colin took her back to bed and, as the Certified Discipline Nymph Jenny would say, ravished her thoroughly for many passion-filled, out-of-control years.

IT'S IN HIS KISS . . .

TURN THE PAGE FOR A PREVIEW OF

P. C. CAST'S NOVEL . . .

GODDESS OF LEGEND

Available in paperback from Berkley Sensation!

✳ 1 ✳

Isabel decided the morning couldn't be more perfect. Well, possibly better if she was sore from a great night of sex, but that wasn't in the cards. Not today, probably not tomorrow. Probably not in this decade. Nonetheless, a beautiful day.

She finished adjusting the tripod that held her favorite camera and then straightened, drawing in a deep breath of the sweet Oklahoma air. She didn't peer through the camera lens as would most photographers. Of course she would eventually, but Isabel trusted her naked eye more than any lens, no matter how clear or magnified or uber-telephoto. So she studied the landscape before her as she sipped from her thermos of Vienna roast coffee.

She caught a glimpse of herself in the silver of her thermos. Distorted as it was, she could tell she was smiling. And her lips, which every lover seemed to comment on, looked like big clown lips. Men seemed to love them. She was always trying to suck them in. She didn't believe for a second that Angelina's were for real. Unfortunately, she knew too well that hers were.

"'When the young dawn, with fingertips of rose lit up the world,'" she murmured, surprising herself with the Homeric quote. "Appropriate, though . . ." Isabel sighed with pleasure. The light here was absolutely exquisite! Oklahoma's Tallgrass Prairie had been the right choice to begin her new photography collection, *American Heartscapes*. It was early spring, but the ridge in front of her was already covered with knee-high grasses, waving oceanlike in the morning breeze. The air had the scent of impending rain, but there were so many more scents that filled her. The grasses, the lake, the occasional odor of a skunk. Nature. What a high.

The sky was an explosion of pastels washed against a backdrop of cumulus clouds that puffed high into the stratosphere—mute testimony to today's weather forecast of midday thunderstorms. Isabel hardly gave the impending storm a thought—she'd be gone before the first raindrop fell. But even if the weather chased her away, she didn't mind. On the ridge before her, under the frothy cotton candy sky, was a sight

Isabel knew would make the perfect cover photo for her collection. The landscape was dotted with bison. Isabel's eyes glistened as she gazed at them, framing pictures—creating art in her mind's eye. The huge beasts looked timeless in the changing light of dawn, especially since they were positioned so that there were no telephone poles or modern houses or even visible roads anywhere around them. It was just the beasts, the land and the amazing sky.

Isabel took another sip of her coffee before she put the cup down and began focusing her camera and setting up the first shots. As she worked, a sense of peace filled her, and Isabel's skin tingled with happiness.

"And you thought you'd lost it," she spoke aloud to herself softly, letting her voice fill the empty space around her. "Well, not lost it," she muttered as she sighted through the telephoto lens and focused on a huge bison bull backlit by the rosebud-hued sky. "Just lost the peace in it."

Ironic, really, that the collection of photographs *USA Today* had called *Peace?* had made her lose her perspective on the subject.

"Afghanistan will do that." Isabel clicked off several frames of the bison.

In retrospect she should have known the assignment was going to be a tough one. But she'd gotten cocky. Hell, she'd been a photojournalist—a successful, award-winning photojournalist—for twenty years now. She wasn't a dewy-eyed twenty-something anymore. She was a fearless forty-two, which was part of her problem. Overconfidence in her ability had blinded her to the realities of what really *seeing* would do to her.

Of course, it wasn't like she hadn't been to war zones before—Bosnia, the Falklands and South Africa had all come before her lens. But something had been different in Afghanistan. *I'd been different. Somehow I'd lost perspective and darkness and chaos slithered in,* Isabel admitted to herself as she changed the angle of the tripod and shot several frames rapidly, catching a young calf frolicking around its grazing mother.

It had started with the soldier, Curtis Johnson. He'd had kind brown eyes set in a face that was young and more cute than handsome. He couldn't have been older than twenty-five, and he'd flirted outrageously with her as he escorted her to the jeep she'd be riding in—the one smack in the middle of the convoy of supplies they were taking from the U.S. airbase to one of the small native settlements just a few miles down the potholed road.

Actually, Curtis had been so cute and clever that she'd been daydreaming about loosening up her rule on not having a fling when she was on assignment. She'd been counting the years between them and had decided that, what the hell, if sexy young Curtis didn't care that she was almost twenty years his senior, then why the hell should she care?

And that was when the roadside bomb detonated. Isabel had switched to photographer autopilot, and in the middle of the smoke and fire, darkness and horror, she'd captured some of the most profound images of her career—images that had included Curtis Johnson, whose strong right leg and well-muscled right arm had been blown completely off. She'd never meant to capture him. She hadn't even realized he'd been part of the blast. She'd meant only to do what was instinctive; capture the truth. And then the truth bombed her in the face, and she nearly fell apart.

Curtis's eyes had still been kind, even as they'd clouded with shock. Before he'd lost consciousness, he'd been worried about her—been warning her to get down . . . get under cover . . . Then he'd bled out on the cracked desert sand and died in her arms. All hell broke loose around her, and all she remembered after that was screaming to keep her camera. She absolutely had to have the pictures of Curtis in life. For his family. For her.

Isabel shivered and realized she'd stopped taking pictures and was standing beside her tripod. She lifted a hand to the chill on her cheeks. They were wet.

"Focus on what you're doing!" Isabel told herself. "This is your chance to regain your center—your normalcy." *And to get over your grief.*

She did the buck-up thing her father had always taught her, got rid of the tears and the memories and focused on her job.

Shaking her head, she returned to the frame of her camera, her smile feeling sarcastic. Her gang of best friends would agree that an Isabel Cantelli norm wasn't anywhere near most people's norm. She could almost hear her gang chastising her. Meredith would shrug and say the Isabel norm usually worked for her—it had certainly made her successful. Robin would shake her head and say Isabel needed to find a full-time man, not just a string of attractive lovers. Kim would dissect Isabel's psyche and eventually agree with Robin that more permanence in her life would help ground her, and Teresa would chime in that whatever made Isabel happy was what she should go for.

Until a month ago and that trip to Afghanistan, Isabel would have laughed, rolled her eyes, poured herself more champagne and said her nomadic life, free of entangling man strings, was exactly what made her happy.

Then Curtis Johnson had happened to her, and Isabel's view of the world had changed, and in this new, tainted viewpoint she'd realized that she'd been fooling herself for quite a while. Or maybe it was more accurate to say that she'd been searching for herself for quite a while, because somewhere in the middle of her successful career and her group of intelligent, articulate friends and her life that was at once exciting and comfortable, she'd lost herself.

Which is why she was here, on Oklahoma's Tallgrass Prairie. She was doing the only thing she knew to reground herself—she was viewing life through her camera and searching for her true north again so she could find a way to navigate through the changing landscape of her life. Her plan had seemed to be working, until she'd allowed her mind to wander and her eyes to see the past. And the past had good and bad memories, times of joy and ridiculous fear. If there was an emotion she'd ever not experienced, she wasn't sure what it would be. She needed something to shock her into enjoyment again. If she could only figure out what it would be. But this, this natural Oklahoma beauty was working right now.

"So focus!" Isabel reminded herself, and was pleased to fall fairly easily back into the zone of framing the lovely land before her.

The next time she moved her tripod, she caught sight of the morning light glistening off the surface of what she realized was water winding through a gully to her right. Intrigued as always by varieties in landscape, she headed in that direction, loving the surprising glimpse of sandy bank and a clear, bubbling stream hidden within the section of cross timbers.

Getting closer to the water, Isabel noticed a single ray of young sunlight had penetrated the green shadows of the trees, so that a small section of the stream was being illuminated, as if by a silver spotlight. That spotlight drew her like a magnet.

She let her instincts guide her, and moved quietly and quickly down the bank, leaving the tripod temporarily behind. As she settled on the sandy ground, kneeling so that she was just above the water, Isabel focused and began clicking picture after picture, changing the angle and distance from the water as she worked. Mesmerized by the unique quality of the light, she let the magic of the lens wash away the sadness thinking of Afghanistan and the fallen soldier had caused. She'd changed position and was lying prone on her stomach, elbows planted in the sand, when the brush on the opposite side of the bank rustled, and accompanied by a massive snapping of twigs, a bison lumbered into view.

Hardly daring to breathe, Isabel kept snapping pictures as the huge beast went to the water. He snorted once at her, probably sensing the scent of an intruder, but then ignored her completely, lowered his black muzzle and drank noisily.

She wondered how she smelled to him. He'd swung his head around until he'd spotted her. She never felt fear, so she didn't believe that's what caught his attention. Did she just smell human? She wasn't wearing perfume, she was lying so still, there was no way he heard her.

What had made him look directly toward her? And why had his eyes seem so ancient and wise? When he backed away from the lake, he shook his head up and down, gave her one more unfathomable look, and then turned and loped away with an agility she'd never have believed of such a huge, amazing beast.

A thrill went through Isabel. She clicked back to glance through the pictures she'd captured of him. The bison had stepped directly into the shaft of light. Morning dew speckled the big bull's coat so that through Isabel's lens he appeared to be swathed in diamonds and mist. And he'd nodded at her. As if he were approving the photo shoot. And as he turned and left, her first thought was that every single human male in existence would give anything for that package he was carrying.

Isabel sat up and laughed aloud with delight, relieved beyond measure that the beauty and peace of this ancient land had begun to do exactly what she'd hoped when she'd discussed this book idea with her agent—it had begun to sooth her soul and help reground her creativity in something more bearable than death and destruction.

Impulsively Isabel kicked off her hiking boots and pulled off her socks. She rolled up her jeans and, still holding her camera, stepped carefully into the crystalline water. Isabel sucked air and gasped at the initial chill, but after a few slow steps, her feet got used to the temperature of the stream, and she made her way to the shaft of sunlight that had so recently framed the bison. When she got to the light, Isabel turned her face up, bathing in the morning's radiance while the cool water washed over her feet and ankles.

There was something about this place that touched her. Maybe it was just the drastic contrast between the calm freedom of the prairie—green, lush and clean—and the war-ravaged Middle East, where everything her eyes had focused on had been dry and burned and in a nightmare of conflict. She breathed deeply—inhaling and exhaling, imagining with every breath she was getting rid of all the negatives within herself and letting the water wash away the remnants of death and war that had clung to her for the past month. Without pausing to wonder why or second-guess whether she was making a fool of herself, Isabel spoke her innermost thoughts aloud to the listening stream and the shaft of light.

"This is just what I need. A new perspective, a new vision. To cleanse myself. That bull was telling me something. He was telling me to go for it. I just wish I knew what 'it' was. Tell me, Lady of the Lake," she said, grinning. "Mrs. Tiger taught us all about you in eighth grade. What is my destiny?"

Isabel knew it was just her imagination, but it seemed the silver light intensified in response to her words, and she could swear she felt a thrill of *something*. Laughing with pleasure, she threw her arms wide and kicked up water so that drops of liquid turned crystal by the sunlight rained around her, baptizing her in brilliance.

Viviane couldn't stay away from her oracle. She knew it was too soon for the tendrils of her magic to have found anyone, but she was filled with frustrated energy. So while her naiads milled nervously around her, the goddess sat in front of her oracle, a crystal basin filled with hundreds of pearls, and fretted.

When a pearl began to glow, she practically pounced on it. Plucking it from the others in the dark, silent batch, she held it up and gazed into its milky depths. The vision cleared to show an old woman sitting beside a large lake, spitting what looked like sunflower seeds into the surf.

"Younger!" Viviane said in disgust, severing the thread and sending it away from the crone. She tossed the pearl back into the basin and began to pace.

The next pearl that lit up showed a child playing beside the ocean. Viviane almost screamed in exasperation. "Not that young!" she admonished her oracle.

The next two visions were utterly unsuitable. Neither were too young or too old, they were just too ordinary. At the end of her already thinly stretched patience, Viviane plucked one long silver strand of silk from the thick fall of hair that hung veil-like around her body. Holding it over the pearl-filled basin, she twirled it in a deceptively lazy circle.

Not too young, old or plain—
with those there is no gain.
Find the perfect woman is my command;
beauty, grace and spirit is what I demand!

The goddess released the strand of her hair, and as the gossamer length floated down into the pearl pool, she completed the spell:

From my own body I lend my oracle power:
find the right soul within this very hour!

There was a flash of silver and the strand of the goddess's

hair exploded, raining sparks of liquid light, which dissolved into the pearls. Invigorated anew, silver threads rushed out from the realm of the goddess and, following seaways and lakes, rivers and streams, they searched through time and realities until one small, glowing thread shot down a tiny waterway in a faraway place called Oklahoma, in the distant, modern mortal world where, in a flash of morning light, it captured the sound of a woman's joyous laughter as she recommitted herself to the bright possibilities in life.

Viviane heard the enticing sound and plucked the glowing pearl. Holding her breath, the goddess peered within the milky depth that cleared to reveal a full-bodied blonde, oddly attired, who was dancing within a cascade of a splashing stream. Viviane's heartbeat increased with excitement.

"Show me her face!" the goddess commanded.

Her oracle tightened on the woman's face. Well, she was certainly attractive. Viviane squinted and focused on her. Not young, but not too old, or at least she didn't appear to be. And there was a definite benefit to a little age and experience. The woman laughed again, and Viviane unexpectedly found her own lips tilting up in response. The sound was musical and it changed the woman from attractive to alluring.

"Yes," Viviane murmured. "I believe she will do quite nicely." The goddess lifted her arms, causing power to swirl around her.

I claim this mortal as fate decrees in her world she dies.
When her life there ends, it will be to me her soul has ties.
My love's sleeping wishes I follow most truly
so that he might escape the despair that binds him so cruelly.
I take nothing that is not already decreed lost;
my purpose is clear—no matter the cost.
Arthur's dour fate shall not come to be
and then my love will return to me!

Then the great water goddess known as Coventina, Merlin's Viviane, hurled a blazing sphere of divine power through her oracle and out . . . out . . . into another time, another place, altering forever fate's plans for Isabel Cantelli.

✳ 2 ✳

Hindsight, Isabel Cantelli decided in hindsight, sucked. She came to this conclusion after steering to avoid a chipmunk and having her SUV spin out of control.

She probably shouldn't have been digging for her dropped cell while she was happily singing "Camelot" and driving sixty on a dirt road. She probably should have let that little dude fend for himself instead of trying to be a hero saving him. Hindsight wasn't fifty-fifty. It was, at the moment, zero-one hundred.

But shoulda, coulda, woulda wasn't going to help her now. She and her Nissan were flying into Grand Lake at an alarming speed.

Isabel braced herself for the swan dive they were about to accomplish, which she doubted would be graceful. The lake, which she'd found magical just minutes ago, was about to kick her in the ass.

So many thoughts raced through her mind. Strangely enough, none of the ones she expected when she knew she was about to die. Her life didn't flash before her eyes; the life she hadn't lived yet did.

Terror, fear of the pain of dying, that all flashed. But the sadness of what she hadn't yet achieved was occupying her brain.

Her car hit the lake with what felt like a nuclear blast. And the air bag had exploded on her, practically trapping her in her seat. When it finally deflated, she tried to unbuckle her seat belt, but for some reason, it wouldn't let go. Since her window had been down, the car was filling up with water and sinking fast.

Unless a miracle showed up, there was no way she would survive. She was on her way to dying, and it was terrifying. Her heart beat desperately, and she knew that wasn't going to last long. She apologized to her heart for letting it down. She apologized to her liver for not mistreating it as much as she could have over the years. What a wasted chance. But even though she thought of friends and family, Isabel's life never passed before her eyes, like so many assure people it will when dying.

Her focus, as her chest squeezed painfully, was all of the

things she hadn't accomplished yet. How could she have forgotten how much more she wanted out of life? The big one was that she'd never found love. Lust, sure. Attraction, sure. But not that elusive thing called true love. To look at a man and know, absolutely, they were meant for each other.

There were many others on her list, but she sure would have liked to experience the feeling of being desperately in love.

Woulda. Coulda. Shoulda.

And then, suddenly, she felt alive again. And she knew, just knew, that somehow, someway, she was being given a second chance.